Teith Bridge, Callander

TRAVEL from Callander to Aberfoyle near Stirling and your route will take you over the charming red bridge crossing the River Teith. The bridge is a replacement for an earlier version dating from 1764 that was thought to be unsuitable for twentieth-century traffic.

The bridge nestles in beautiful scenery in an area of the Trossachs National Park. It's a lovely spot where Callander Crags, to the north, mark the Highland Boundary Fault, dividing the Scottish Highlands from the Lowlands. This location means that nearby Callander town is often known as the "gateway to the Highlands".

The town has a long history. In the sixth century, St Kessog, a follower of St Columba, lived and taught here. The area continued to be relatively peaceful until 1645 when it was the site of a battle between warring clans, the Campbells of Argyll and the McGregors and McNabs. A more recent claim to fame arose in the 1960s when Callander served as the location for the BBC television series "Dr Finlay's Casebook". ∎

Contents

Dear Readers . . .

I'm delighted to welcome you to "The People's Friend" Annual 2018. Its 176 pages are packed with hours of feel-good reading, with 25 heartwarming new short stories written by some of your favourite authors and accompanied by beautiful colour illustrations.

We've included a selection of seasonal poems to suit every mood and occasion, 10 glorious watercolour paintings from the brush of J. Campbell Kerr, and a nostalgic look back at some of the brightest and best-loved stars of the silver screen.

I do hope you enjoy reading it all!

Angela

Angela Gilchrist, Editor

p57

Poetry

J. Campbell Kerr Paintings

Stars Of Our Screen

Around The Bells

by Anne Stenhouse

THERE was a crisp layer of frost as Archie trudged up the hill from the shops in the village main street. He was glad, because first footing in the rain was a miserable business. It was much better in the cold. A pair of heavy shoes instead of wellies made a visitor more welcome when the ladies had been to such trouble cleaning their houses for the big night.

Tonight would be the biggest night any of them would ever experience. New Year's Eve, 1999.

He reached his mother's house and wondered what stage her preparations would be at.

As soon as the door swung back he smelled potato and leek soup. How good that had been to come in to when they'd all been round the village as teenagers.

"Hello, Mum. Sam sent me up with this tray of vol-au-vents," he called from the front door.

It was a bit of a struggle balancing the tray and trying to wiggle his key out of the lock, but he managed it in the end.

"Vol-au-vents?" his mum asked as she emerged from the kitchen at the end of the hall. "What are they when they're at home?"

"You know, little savoury pastry things," Archie replied, rising to her teasing.

"Vol-au-vents were the big thing in the Seventies," Mrs Prentice said. "Is Sam keen on them?"

"She saw a recipe for retro treats. You were still making them when I was wee. Oh, and I stopped into the Co-op to buy some cans of beer for you."

"Thanks, I forget you young folk prefer beer. A dram was your dad's tipple." Mrs Prentice accepted the tray and Archie stashed the beer in the fridge.

"We thought we might look in after the bells . . ."

"After the bells? So I'm to be here on my own when the lights go out, am I?" Mrs Prentice said with a grin.

Archie laughed.

"You haven't been reading that stuff about the computer programmes failing, have you? Some of my staff are in a right twitter about that."

Her answering smile lit up her face.

Illustration by Ruth Blair.

"We'll see. Thank Sam for the pastries. How is she feeling?"

"She's having a rest at the minute, otherwise she would have come over to help with the table. Still three weeks till her due date, and she's put on a lot of –"

"Girth?" Mrs Prentice supplied. "I know what you mean. She's bigger than her sisters at the same stage in their pregnancies. You are remembering her dad was a twin?"

"No, I'm seriously trying to bury that fact. Sam's had scans and it is one baby only."

When his mum still looked unconvinced, Archie went on.

"She'll be fine." He took the lid from the big stock pot and smelled the soup. "Need a taster?"

*   *   *   *

Sam was up and about when Archie got back to their flat above his father-in-law's garage. She was moving with a slow grace despite the size of her bump and his heart swelled.

Only a few more weeks and they'd know whether they had a boy or a girl.

Archie didn't care as much as Sam's dad. Mr Drummond was desperate for a grandson. After three daughters and five granddaughters, he regarded it as his due. Sam was a biology teacher and she could only shake her head when he voiced this opinion.

"Did you sleep?" Archie asked.

"A little. Mum phoned to remind us they would be at Jilly's if anything happened."

"And woke you?"

His wife nodded ruefully.

"I didn't understand how much this baby belongs to everyone," she said. "Is your mum organised? Will there be an Eightsome Reel in the street like last year?" Sam rubbed her back as she spoke and, as Archie watched, a tiny grimace clouded her face.

"Sam?" he asked nervously.

"It's nothing. Been happening for days now. Braxton Hicks contractions. Remember, I told you . . ."

"Yes, miss." He crossed the room and pulled her towards him. "We don't have to go first footing, you know. We could curl up here with the telly on and watch folk in Edinburgh at the fireworks."

"Nonsense. Who would eat your mum's soup?"

"No shortage of neighbours who'll be looking in for that. Seriously, love, if you don't feel up to it, just say." His words faded away as he yawned.

"Look at you. Did your mum have you cleaning the pelmets again?"

"This year she's focusing on the backs of the furniture. We shifted two wardrobes, and even empty wardrobes are heavy," Archie said with feeling.

He couldn't understand this passion the women had for going into the New Year with a clean house.

"As if any spider would dare to take up residence behind her furniture – Sam!" Archie caught his wife as she sank to her knees.

"Oh, Archie," she managed as a wave of pain etched itself on her features. "I wonder if she'll be the first baby born in St Joseph's in the new millenium?"

*　　*　　*　　*

"We came as quickly as we could, Mrs Prentice." Archie heard his father-in-law's voice in the hospital corridor. "Every junction seemed to be twice as clogged up as usual. How are things going?"

"Much as they would want, the doctor said. She came out a few minutes ago and spoke to Archie and me before she went on to the next girl. She's Polish."

"The doctor?"

"No. The doctor is Sadie Watts who was three years above Sam at school."

"Sadie Watts," Sam's mum interrupted. "I didn't know she'd come back from Newcastle."

"So, who's Polish, then?" Bert Drummond asked.

Archie thought it was just typical. Here they were at the most important moment of their lives and the in-laws were fretting over details.

He patted Sam's hand and went out into the corridor.

"Hello, folks. Sam's good, but it's getting quite close now. Do you think you could all go along to the family room?" he asked without much hope of getting any peace for Sam in the last hour or so of her labour. "In fact, why don't you all go down to Mum's and I'll phone as soon as I can?"

"We've just got here, Archie," Mr Drummond complained. "And you've no idea what the traffic was like around the supermarket in Livingston."

"Sorry, I just think Mum needs to get back for the phone calls." He sent his mum an appealing glance and she rose to the occasion.

"Of course. How silly of me."

"Right," Bert said. "Phone calls?"

"My daughters are both in New Zealand this year. They always phone at midnight Scottish time, though, wherever they are in the world."

"We can drive you down," Mr Drummond said as he opened the clasp on his sporran to reach his keys. "Good job we'd been dancing and not toasting yet."

"May I just take a wee peep?" Sam's mum asked, and without waiting for an answer ducked into the labour room.

She was as good as her word, though, and came out again very quickly.

"Everything OK?" Mr Drummond asked, and when his wife reassured him they went off to settle in to wait for the New Year and Archie's phone call.

He made it at 11.36 p.m.

"Mum, it's a lassie. A beautiful wee girl. We're going to call her Ellen." Archie was crying and had to take a breath before he carried on. "Oh, Mum!"

"Congratulations, Archie. A girl. That's lovely."

Archie listened as a cheer went up in his mum's living-room.

"Who have you got there, then?"

"Loads of folk. Never mind them. Janet needs to know how Sam is. I'll give her the phone."

Archie heard a bit of shuffling going on and then his mother-in-law came on the line.

"How's Sam?"

"She's good, Mrs Drummond. Really good." Archie knew the relief in his voice would tell Mrs Drummond more than the words he spoke.

It had been a nerve-shredding climax to the century for the Prentices. He realised his mother-in-law was asking about the Polish girl. She would want to know everything was all right there, too, so she could enjoy Sam's good news.

"The Polish girl? Yes, she's had a boy. It's really busy on the ward," he was adding when the door of Sam's room opened and a nurse stuck her head through.

"What?" Archie held the phone away from his ear when the doctor also came into the corridor. He could hardly credit what she was telling him. "Mrs

Drummond, they need me back in the ward. I'll ring again."

He hoped more than ever that all the hype about failing computer programmes was just that.

*   *   *   *

Archie knew that, down in the village, the family would be pouring drinks in these last minutes before the bells. His mum would be putting the television on and everyone would be gathering in the living-room, except tall, dark Mr Williamson from two doors down.

He'd be lurking in the frost with a bit of coal wrapped up in newspaper in one pocket and a bottle of whisky in the other. It was so familiar, yet this year it was going to be so different. He suppressed a squeal as Sam's hand crushed his fingers.

Just as the midwife allowed Sam to push, he spared a thought for his father-in-law. Not only had 1999 brought him another granddaughter, but it also looked as if it was going to bring him two.

At 20 past midnight on January 1, 2000, the lights, and everything else, were working in St Joseph's hospital.

Archie stepped out under a covered walkway. He looked over to Edinburgh and saw the sky full of fireworks and the glow of a big city well lit up.

He drew a deep breath and hoped he was composed enough to speak to his mum.

"Happy New Year, darling. How are your lovely girls?"

"They're fine, although Ellen's nose might be a bit out of joint," he said. "We have a son, too."

"It was twins?"

"Yes! Ellen has a twin brother and he was born after the bells, and in another century to boot! We think we'll call him Josh Robert."

Archie heard the chaos in his mum's front room as the word went round. Within seconds Mr Drummond was on the phone.

"Archie, is it right? Do we hae a boy?"

Archie thought Mr Drummond had already enjoyed a dram or two, but he couldn't resist teasing him a wee bit.

"*Gratulacje*! *Szczesliwego Nowego Roku.*"

"You've got me there, Archie."

"It's Polish. Sam's neighbour in the labour ward had a boy and that's what her man said to me. It means 'Congratulations. Happy New Year'."

"Does it now?" Mr Drummond wasn't overly interested in the international dimension. "It's down to me, you know. I'm the twin."

Archie laughed. As he watched the glow over the village its lights went off. They came on again within seconds, but the trip in the system guaranteed Mrs Prentice's New Year party a place in village folklore. ∎

Illustration by Jim Dewar.

Little Tinker

by Vivien Hampshire

THE day that Tinker turned up in my back garden, unannounced and decidedly bedraggled, was otherwise unremarkable.

I'd sat around after a late breakfast, still in my dressing-gown, skimming through the newspaper and wondering why I bothered still to buy one when all that was in it was more and more trouble in the world and pages of celebrity gossip.

Then I'd had another cup of tea, pulled on my old gardening clothes and wandered outside to do some much-needed deadheading.

I was bored. Having accepted an early-retirement package three months earlier – the alternative being relocation to the new company offices almost 200 miles away – I still hadn't found anything to fill my days.

It was hard, after 35 years of getting up to the sound of an alarm, dressing for the office and catching the train at 8.20 every morning, to find myself with time on my hands and absolutely no structure to my daily life at all.

My sister Lorna insisted that I would get used to it soon enough and that there were huge benefits to be gained from being your own boss, as she laughingly called it. Holidays at the drop of a hat; meeting friends for coffee; having a lie-in whenever I fancied one and not having to go out at all when it snowed!

She made it sound like I'd been missing out on something wonderful all these years. The reality was that I missed my old life – the people, the sense of purpose, the responsibility.

Rattling about at home with all the housework done and not even a good book to read until my next trip to the library, I felt more than a little sorry for myself.

They say that life has a habit of giving you what you need when you least expect it, don't they? That you don't have to go looking for luck. If it's meant to be, it will find you.

And that's how it was with Tinker. Snipping away with my secateurs, humming to break the silence and with my mind miles away in an office that no longer existed, I didn't hear his plaintive little cries at first. In fact, if he hadn't jumped out of the way as I bent down to lop off a few dead brown leaves hanging close to the ground, I could easily have had his tail off, poor little mite.

I wasn't familiar with kittens. Growing up, there had been a succession of family dogs and, until it found a hole in the fence and disappeared without trace, a tortoise called Timmy we'd inherited from an elderly neighbour.

Cats were a mystery. I admired them for their haughtiness and independence, the fact they didn't need constant attention or twice-daily walks, and the way they pretty much took care of themselves.

But this little fellow didn't look capable of taking care of himself at all. He was small. I judged him to be only a couple of months old, and when I picked him up – tentatively in case he decided to lash out with his claws – he fitted easily into the palm of my hand with just his front paws hanging over the side.

He was mainly black, with a splodge of white under his tummy and at the tip of one ear. And he was thin. Running my finger down his back, I could feel his tiny bones through the matted fur and saw what looked like fleas hopping about around his neck. It was obvious he had been outside for some time.

"Well, now, young Tinker," I said, speaking softly to make sure I didn't frighten him. "Where have you come from?"

I have no idea why I called him Tinker, but the name seemed to suit him.

"Let's take you inside, shall we, and find you something to eat?"

I carried him through to the kitchen, surprised to realise how quickly he had accepted me. By the time I sat down at the table and spooned some tuna into the saucer still left out from my earlier cup of tea, he was already rubbing his head against my arm and purring fit to burst.

He guzzled the tuna down and followed it with a slice of honey roast ham. It was the best I could do at short notice, but he didn't seem to mind.

Then he scampered across the kitchen floor and into the lounge, managed to jump up into my favourite armchair and fell fast asleep. Talk about making himself at home!

I had forgotten all about my gardening efforts and turned my thoughts towards what I should do with my unexpected visitor when he woke up. Get him checked over at the vet? Try to find out if anyone locally might have lost him, or take him to some kind of rescue centre?

The last thing on my mind was to keep him. But keep him I did!

*　　*　　*　　*

The vet looked him over the next morning, confirmed he was indeed a male, sold me some flea treatment and searched for a microchip that wasn't there.

The receptionist put a *Found: Kitten* notice on the board and directed me to a website for lost and found pets. I popped him back into the cardboard box I had used to transport him there and took him home, where he promptly went straight back to sleep, giving me time to dash to the supermarket and stock up on cat food before he woke up again.

I bought a plastic litter tray and a bag of litter while I was there. Up till now we'd got by with a sprinkling of garden soil on a pile of old newspapers, but it wasn't ideal, and if I wanted to keep my kitchen floor clean then these things would have to be done properly.

It wasn't until three days later that it occurred to me Tinker had actually moved in. Not as a temporary guest, but for ever. Nobody had reported him missing, nobody responded to the notice at the vet's.

I hadn't got around to calling the rescue centre. What would they do, anyway? Try to find him a new home, and keep him in a cage until they did? Tinker didn't need a new home. He had found one, with me.

After that, life became a lot less boring with a little furry face nudging me awake every morning and a warm body curled on my lap every time I sat down. It felt good to have someone to care for and to talk to. The house felt less empty, and I found myself looking forward to the future and making plans again.

*　　*　　*　　*

"I thought you didn't like cats!" Lorna said on her next visit.

"I never said I didn't like them. I just never had a lot to do with them before."

She had brought her grandchildren with her. Lily and Sean were eight-year-old twins, bursting with energy and curiosity. I hadn't had a lot to do with children in the past, either, never having had any of my own, but I'd soon come to love these two, as I now pointed out to my sister.

"That's different," she said. "They're not animals; they're family."

I looked at little Tinker, chasing a ball of wool he'd pulled from my knitting bag, and smiled. He wasn't just an animal, he was family, too, now. But it would have been pointless trying to explain that to Lorna.

"Anyway, I've decided to visit that animal rescue place in Little Oakford."

Lorna stopped drinking her tea and put her cup down.

"What for? I thought you'd decided to keep him."

"I have. Or, more like, he's decided to keep me!"

"Then what do you want with animal rescue? Not going to start taking in waifs and strays, are you?" Lorna snorted.

"Probably not. But if there's one thing this little chap has taught me, it's that no animal should be without a loving home. And no lonely person should be without a loving pet. I'm going to volunteer my services, and try to do something about matching the two up. I hear they're always looking for volunteers, and with my office experience and time on my hands, it might suit me."

"Are you sure you wouldn't rather spend more time in the garden, or write your memoirs or something? Maybe go on a relaxing cruise?"

I laughed.

"I'm sick of the garden, I've never done anything exciting to write about and I get seasick just crossing the Channel on the ferry to France! I need more purpose in my life, Lorna. Tinker turned up here for a reason, I'm sure of it."

"Yes – he recognised a soft touch when he saw one! Free food and a comfy bed. I think I would have done the same in his position."

"You've got Harry and the kids." I watched the twins rolling around the floor with Tinker, slowly twisting the yards of unravelling wool into knots I would never be able to untangle. "Life is different for you. Tinker has filled a hole in mine that I hadn't even realised was there. Maybe I can do the same for someone else. It's worth a try, don't you think?"

On that note, before she could pour cold water on any more of my plans, I gathered up the empty cups and left the room.

∗   ∗   ∗   ∗

The rescue centre was much smaller than I had imagined. Hidden behind a high wire fence, it consisted of a rather tatty Portakabin with a sign above its creaky door saying *Reception. Please come in*, an equally dilapidated portable loo and a series of assorted huts and pens arranged higgledy-piggledy across an area hardly bigger than my own back garden.

14

"Hello, can I help you?" An elderly red-faced woman looked up as I knocked gently and poked my head around the door.

"I hope so. Although I was rather hoping it's me who might be able to help you! I'm Jan Roberts. I'd like to find out about offering my services in some way. Just a couple of days a week, maybe?"

"Oh, how lovely! Please do come in and sit down. I'm Rose Garner, the manager here. Manager sounds rather grand – truth is I'm sort of head animal-keeper, accountant, fund-raiser and phone-answerer all rolled into one. Any help is very much appreciated, I can assure you. You do realise we can't pay?"

"Of course. I'm not looking for money, just something useful to do."

"Recently retired?"

"How did you guess?"

"Been there and done that." Rose laughed. "Got the T-shirt, as they say."

I was going to like Rose, I could tell.

"Let me show you around before you commit yourself to anything. We're quite basic, low on facilities, if you know what I mean, and run off our feet a lot of the time. We're totally reliant on voluntary contributions, both of cash and time, but it's very rewarding. I take it you like animals? Silly question, but it is rather important that you do. Do you have any pets of your own?"

My mind flipped to Tinker, who I'd left curled up at the end of my bed with a full bowl of meaty chunks awaiting him in the kitchen. I never could have done that with a dog, but my little Tinker was already showing that feline independent streak I had always admired, and I knew he'd be fine by himself for a few hours.

"Yes, I do. He's the reason I'm here. Let's say that he's managed to open my eyes to a few things lately."

Rose walked me around each of the outbuildings and introduced me to various cats, dogs, rabbits and hamsters.

"They don't generally stay here long," she explained. "We try very hard to rehome them as soon as we possibly can. But there are more animals arriving every week – lost, abandoned, no longer wanted, sometimes hurt. Mostly domestic pets, but we do see the occasional wild animal. A baby owl, or an injured fox. Someone brought us in a swan a while back with a broken leg."

She sighed.

"It can be hard to let them go once we get attached to them, but a good recovery and a for-ever home is what we're ultimately aiming for, for all of our residents. In ninety per cent of cases we achieve it."

"And the other ten?"

"They stay here. For as long as they need."

The more I saw, the more I knew I wanted to get involved.

"So, what can I do to help? I'm no animal expert, but I'm good with a computer. Paperwork, files, that sort of thing."

"Well, I'm no office expert and I'd much rather be out here with the animals, so it seems to me we'd make a pretty good team! When can you start?"

*   *   *   *

I went every Wednesday and Friday after that, and soon had the small office running like clockwork, popping outside to help with feeding and dog-walking whenever things were quiet or I needed a break from the paperwork.

As I was a volunteer, there was no pressure. I could choose my own hours and walk away at any time if I felt like it. Not that I ever did. The rescue centre started to feel like my second home, and Tinker, growing bigger and bolder every day, was always there to welcome me at the end of the day.

I did worry that he might be lonely, but a beautiful little stray cat called Sheri soon solved that problem for me.

"Are you sure, Jan?" Rose asked when I presented her with the rehoming forms, already signed with my own name. "It's easy to get involved with the animals here. Before you know it, you'll want to take all of them home!"

But I was sure.

Sheri soon made herself very much at home and, being older, was quick to take on the role of mother and boss where little Tinker was concerned. Often I would come home to find them curled up together at the end of my bed or sharing a bowl of food, nose to nose. They rarely scrapped, although chasing around the place at high speed became a favourite game and I had to move a few ornaments and vases out of the way, to make sure they didn't get broken.

Now the cats were happy in each other's company and starting to explore their new garden with easy access through their newly installed cat flap, I felt able to spend more time at the centre. I soon added Thursdays to my regular shifts.

Thursday was the one day of the week that Simon Grey came in as a volunteer. I'd heard his name, of course, from some of the others, but our paths hadn't crossed before. Now he stood in front of me, wearing an old jacket and a pair of huge green wellies. He had a bag of straw hefted over his shoulder.

"Pleased to meet you at last, Jan." He shook my hand and laid the straw down. "It's you we have to thank for sorting out the office, I understand. So nice to be able to find the right forms and not have to fight my way through the mounds of paper that used to litter the place. You must be some kind of miracle worker!"

I blushed. I might be in my fifties, but compliments were still a surprise.

"Not at all. Just organised after years of office work, and glad to keep my hand in now that part of my life is over. How about you? Are you retired, too?"

He nodded.

"Police force, but I took retirement a couple of years back. Coming here gets me out in the fresh air and gives me a bit of exercise. I'm not one for the gym

– far too boring. Besides, I like the animals. I used to handle police dogs, and always had one at home with me. But since I lost Elsie . . ."

"Your wife?"

"No. Elsie was my last dog. A real beauty. Retired with me, but died just six months ago, poor thing. No, there's no wife. Never met the right woman!"

I saw a lot of Simon after that. He was there every Thursday, working outdoors most of the time, but he'd usually pop into the little cabin for a coffee mid-morning, and sit and chat for a while. It was he who told me about the old tortoise that had just been brought in. Someone had found it wandering at the bottom of their garden and didn't know how to look after it.

"We'll happily do that for you," Simon had told them, taking the large cardboard box and peering inside. "Wow, he's a beauty, and no mistake!"

Simon put the box on the desk in front of me as he drank his coffee.

"I'll leave the old fellow here for a short while if that's OK with you, while I sort him out some proper living quarters and some food."

When he'd gone, I looked inside. There was something calming about a tortoise. Slow and plodding, as if there was nothing worth hurrying for.

This one was big, with very distinctive markings on his shell, and he was munching on a cabbage leaf, quite unperturbed about finding himself in this new and strange environment.

I smiled. He reminded me very much of old Timmy, the tortoise we'd briefly had and lost when I was a girl. He'd had markings just like these.

In fact, the more I looked at him, the more I began to convince myself that this was Timmy. But surely that couldn't be, could it? Not after 40 years?

There were some animal books on the shelves. I'd catalogued them all not so long ago, and sorted them into order, according to animal type and breed.

It took seconds to lay my hands on the tortoise book, and soon I was absorbed in reading all about these magnificent creatures.

Tortoises are one of the longest lived animals. They can live up to one hundred and fifty years. They don't travel very fast or very far.

"Simon!" I gabbled as soon as he came back into the room. "I lost a tortoise just like this one once. Do you think it's possible that this could be him? The markings are just the same."

"Slow down, Jan. Start at the beginning. There's no rush. This one isn't going anywhere in a hurry!"

I was being silly, of course. There was no way of proving the tortoise's identity, of knowing where he had come from or how long he had been lost.

But I knew, just as I had with Sheri, that I had to have him.

"I want to take him home with me, Simon."

"Well, wouldn't you like to think about it first?"

"No! Please don't bother settling him into a pen. I have a huge back garden for him to live in, and with the help of this book I can make sure he gets the right things to eat, and . . ."

"And a proper shelter to hibernate in? And foolproof fencing so he can't escape again?"

"OK. I know I have a lot to learn, but if it is Timmy I feel I owe it to him."

"And if it isn't?"

"Well, I want him anyway."

"In that case, if you're sure, we'll get the rehoming forms filled in, run it past Rose and I will personally escort you both home. I can inspect the garden fence for you, and help to plug up any gaps. How does that sound?"

"Perfect. But on one condition."

"Which is?"

"That you stay for dinner."

*   *   *   *

Lorna almost drops her biscuit as she splutters crumbs in disbelief.

"You've what?" she says.

"I've started dating," I say again. "His name is Simon."

"That's what I thought you said. Well, you're a dark horse, aren't you?"

I feel Tinker jump up on to my lap. Sheri tries to do the same to my sister.

"Get down," she says, brushing the cat away. "You'll get hairs on my skirt."

"She doesn't mean any harm."

"Honestly, Jan, this house is turning into some kind of menagerie lately. I'm dreading what might turn up next! Which brings me back to what we were just talking about before this . . . this animal interrupted us. Now, tell me all about this elusive Simon. And when am I going to meet him?"

"Any minute now, actually. He's dropping by with Molly."

"Molly? Who's Molly?"

"His puppy. He's only recently got her from the centre. A sweet little mongrel nobody else seemed to want. But we did."

"We? So, it's we already, is it?"

I think ahead to the day when we will merge our lives, our homes and our pets together under one very warm and welcoming roof.

Simon has asked me to marry him. It seems he has met the right woman at last, and I know for certain that I've met the right man. All we have to do now is introduce Molly to Timmy and the cats, and get their seal of approval.

Hopefully they'll accept her and love her as easily as they did each other.

"It's always going to be 'we' from now on, Lorna," I tell my sister.

I pick Tinker up from my lap to rub his little white-tipped ear.

If it weren't for him turning up on that unremarkable day, none of the ...te remarkable changes that followed would ever have happened.

"In fact, thanks to this little minx and the joy he has brought into my life," I say as I hear the doorbell ring, "I don't think I will ever feel lonely again." ∎

Bamburgh Castle, Northumberland

AN ancient volcano erupting off what is now the Northumbrian coast left a legacy in the form of a rocky outcrop that made a perfect defensive position for a castle. Sure enough, when the area became populated, it wasn't long before the locals sought to make the most of this natural advantage.

The earliest written record of the castle comes from AD 547 when Ida of Bernicia (the old name for the area) captured the site and made it his royal seat. A couple of generations later and his grandson, Aethelfrith, passed the castle on to his wife, Bebbe. It became known as Bebbanburgh (Bebbe's town) and from there we get the modern name of Bamburgh.

That castle is long gone – the Vikings destroyed the original – but the site was redeveloped by the Normans with the beginnings of what is now Bamburgh Castle.

The imposing structure, with views along the coast and to the Farne Islands, has become familiar from its use as a location in film productions including "A Connecticut Yankee In King Arthur's Court" with Danny Kaye, and the popular 1980s TV series "Robin Of Sherwood", starring Michael Praed as Robin Hood. ■

My Valentine's Birthday

by Suzanne Ross Jones

EVERYONE will be here by seven tomorrow night, Val," Mum told me as she put the finishing touches to my cake. "So make sure you're home in plenty of time."

"Everyone?" I asked faintly. It hadn't even occurred to me my birthday would be a family gathering now I was no longer a child.

"Yes," she replied with a smile. "And the party will be able to run on even later than usual now you're older."

"But seventeen isn't a special birthday."

She smiled.

"Every birthday's special. Besides, these gatherings are tradition. Everyone expects to be here to help you celebrate."

I didn't need to ask who everyone was. I had a large collection of aunts and uncles and, as the only child in a career-orientated family, I'd become the focus of everyone's interest.

I suspected the gatherings weren't so much for me any longer, but an excuse for everyone to keep a date in their busy lives to get together. And it was a given I would be in for an evening of fun and laughter and being fussed over.

There was only one problem.

As I looked at Mum's happy face, I knew I couldn't tell her. She always put so much work into organising my parties.

This was the first time I realised just how inconvenient having a birthday on Valentine's Day could be. It hadn't occurred to anyone that I might have made plans of my own this year.

"I'm so sorry," I told Eddie when I saw him later. "I can't go out with you tomorrow night after all."

His face fell and I felt terrible. He'd booked a table at a really posh restaurant in town for us to celebrate my birthday and our first Valentine's Day as a couple. He'd been saving up for ages, too, so he could treat me.

"Why not?"

When I told him, he smiled.

"Not to worry. I'm sure they'll be able to find someone to fill the booking. We

Illustration by Jim Dewar.

can go out for dinner another time."

Just like that, he let me off the hook. That's when I knew I'd found a keeper.

My birthday that year was the first time he'd met Mum and Dad and the others. And, because of that, it had to be one of the most memorable Valentine's Days ever.

* * * *

There was no chance of a romantic celebration on our second Valentine's Day together, either.

"I'm sorry," I told Eddie. "They've arranged the biggest party known to humankind."

It seemed Mum had been planning my eighteenth birthday from the day I was born, so who was I to complain?

At least I didn't complain to Mum. But I had a good grumble to Eddie as we walked arm in arm in the park the Saturday before.

"Other families don't go overboard for every birthday," I told him. "So why do mine? And why couldn't I have a birthday on any other day of the year?"

"It's much better that they're making a fuss, rather than not bothering at all."

He was right, of course, and I was reminded again of how lucky I was to be with him. I nodded my agreement and he drew me close and kissed my nose.

"Why don't we have a Valentine's lunch instead?" he suggested.

I shook my head.

"There's no need. We'll see each other at the party."

"Please?" he asked. "I want to spoil you."

Lunch didn't have the same ring to it as a romantic candlelit dinner, but it would have to do.

$$* \quad * \quad * \quad *$$

So lunch became our Valentine's thing. And our Valentine's evenings were spent with my family, celebrating my birthday.

"Don't you ever want to spend a romantic Valentine's with Dad?" I asked Mum the following year as she iced the cake. "I wouldn't mind."

She smiled.

"We can enjoy romantic dinners any time, but you only have one birthday. We'd much rather spend it with you."

My hint had not been taken up.

And so Eddie and I kept to our celebration lunches.

He proposed at our fifth romantic lunch and we were married exactly a year later – though it meant our romantic lunch became a sit-down wedding breakfast for 80 that year. And my birthday celebration doubled as our evening do.

As the best man toasted the bride and groom, I smiled, sure that now we were married we'd be able to set our own agendas for celebrating my birthday.

I was wrong.

"How wonderful," my aunt said, red-faced from one too many glasses of champagne. "Now we'll be able to celebrate your anniversary as well as your birthday."

"But Valentine's Day's supposed to be for lovers," I told Eddie. "Not for the whole family."

"We have all year round to be romantic," he told me as he held me tight and twirled me around for our first dance. "We can share your birthday – and Valentine's – with your family. It obviously means so much to them."

"Oh, that's a lovely thing to say." I hugged him. "We are romantic every day, aren't we?"

$$* \quad * \quad * \quad *$$

Once the children arrived, I could understand exactly why my family had been so keen for our get-togethers on my birthday. There's nothing quite like sharing a child's joy as they blow out their birthday candles. Or seeing their faces beaming as everyone sings "Happy Birthday".

Mum, Dad, my aunts and uncles, now all retired from work, joined us for our children's celebrations. And Jack, aged four, and Abigail, two, revelled in all the attention. Just as I had done as a child.

Despite this, they still wanted to get together on my birthday, too. I still didn't

Spring's Return

MORNING is dawning,
A new day's arriving,
Skies are now clearing
And sunrise is due;
Delicate patterns streak out
On the skyline
Then fade, to allow
A vista of blue.
Sunshine bursts out
To envelop the spectrum,
Golden and glowing,
In radiant light;
Heralds the visit
Of springtime's returning,
Days that will lengthen
And stay warm and bright!

– Elizabeth Gozney.

have the heart to disappoint them.

Besides, these days I barely gave a thought to my missed romantic Valentine's dinners, though Eddie and I did manage still to sneak out for lunch together.

And, as the years passed, that became just as much a tradition for us as my birthday get-togethers were for my family.

*   *   *   *

Then, one year, Mum arranged my party from her hospital bed. Birthday celebrations were the last thing on anyone's mind, but it was what she wanted.

"Do you want to go for lunch?" Eddie asked that morning.

I shook my head.

"Do you mind if we don't this year? I'd rather eat here – just you, me and the children."

He nodded and lifted Abigail on to his knee and kissed the top of her head.

He obviously felt as I did – that he wanted our family close.

Mum was allowed home for a few hours after the doctor's afternoon rounds. Despite the fact she was so delicate, I'd never seen her look so happy as she did when I blew out my birthday candles.

It was a memory we cherished.

iStock.

23

The following year was the hardest. There was a big gaping hole in our lives.

"There won't be a party this year," I told Eddie. "Not when Mum's not here to arrange it."

"Family's important more than ever now. Carrying on with your birthday parties is what your mum would have wanted you to do."

It wasn't a party, but we all went around to Dad's. We sat drinking tea and sharing memories.

Eddie and I missed our lunch that year, too, but he held my hand tightly as the obligatory, if subdued, chorus of "Happy Birthday" rang out. I was more grateful than ever for his love and support.

That was the meaning of romance for me: someone who was there for me, as Eddie always was.

*　　*　　*　　*

Over time, we learned to live with our loss. Mum was always in my heart, of course she was, but I no longer expected to see her when I went round to Dad's, or to hear her voice whenever the phone rang.

It was up to me to arrange the parties now, and I did so in her memory. Rather than just Valentine's or birthday celebrations, these gatherings became more than the sum of the parts and were now a continuation of the tradition Mum had started.

Once Dad moved to a smaller place, our get-togethers happened at our house. It made more sense, particularly as our house on the hill was remote and we were less likely to disturb the neighbours with countless cars and noisy late-evening goodbyes.

Before I knew it, our children had grown up and left home. But they always came back for my birthday.

"If you'd prefer to spend the day with your sweethearts, I won't mind," I told them, remembering how I'd felt all those years ago.

"Don't be silly, Mum," Abigail told me, giving me a hug. "I wouldn't miss your party for the world."

"Would it be OK, though," Jack asked a little hesitantly, "if I brought someone this year?"

I smiled, knowing it was serious if he was bringing his girlfriend to meet the family.

*　　*　　*　　*

"Look at that," Eddie said as he balanced the breakfast tray on the dressing table and threw open the curtains to reveal a winter wonderland. "That snow looks deep."

It did. There was no way anyone would be able to drive up our hill today, and it would be too difficult for most of our guests to walk.

"My party!" I said faintly. "And our lunch. Why didn't we ever buy that four-wheel drive we kept talking about?"

"Because we've only ever been snowed in once in over twenty years in this house," he reminded me. "And that was over Christmas."

I smiled, remembering those few days very well.

He moved the breakfast tray on to the bed.

"Happy birthday." He leaned in for my birthday kiss.

We spent the morning phoning around to cancel the party. Everyone was disappointed, but agreed it couldn't be helped.

"It looks like we might finally get that romantic Valentine's meal alone after all these years." Eddie squeezed my hand.

The fact we still wanted to share a romantic Valentine's dinner, even after more than 30 years together, was something to be very grateful for.

As the day wore on, though, I couldn't help being disappointed. I'd so been looking forward to seeing my family all together. Dad, aunts, uncles, my own children, plus the possibility of a new addition to the family in Jack's first serious girlfriend.

"We can rearrange," Eddie told me. "We'll ask them all round when this snow clears up."

I nodded.

"Good idea."

But it wouldn't be the same. All my adult life I'd spent Valentine's Day wanting to be alone with Eddie, but it was only now I realised how lucky I'd been to be surrounded by all the people who loved me most in the world – not just my husband.

"Cup of tea?" Eddie asked and I nodded.

He went through to the kitchen and seconds later called to me.

"I'm just going out to fetch some milk."

"I bought some the other day." We had lots of milk – enough for a party full of people. But it was too late; he'd gone. And he was ages.

I was about to set out as a search party of one when he came back.

"Quickly, get your coat," he said. "I've borrowed a four by four from work. It's at the bottom of the hill. The roads aren't too bad in the village and it's a tight squeeze in his bungalow, but I've managed to get everyone to your dad's. Abigail and Jack and his girlfriend went straight there from the station."

"Really?" I grinned. "But what about our romantic evening together?"

He threw back his head and laughed.

"Every day with you is Valentine's Day, my love. But I could see you were unhappy about missing your party."

Suddenly the bogus milk run made sense. My one true Valentine had gone out of his way to give me the day I wanted.

That had to be the most romantic Valentine's gesture of all. ■

Where The River Leads

by Wendy Clarke

THE river pulls Eva with it, drawing her towards the sea.
All around her, swimmers in their blue hats forge ahead, their hands dipping into the brown water, their legs sending out a stream of ripples behind them. She's tried too hard from the start; swum too fast.

She should never have tried to keep up with the others. Should never have tried to keep up with Jennifer.

Gasping for breath, Eva raises her chin to stop the salty water splashing into her mouth as the bodies in their black wetsuits pass by. Every now and again an official in a yellow canoe, paddles dripping water and weed, carves a path through the water next to her, but soon they, too, have pulled ahead.

In front of her is the stone bridge. The halfway point.

The bank slopes gently at this point, the muddy edges tasselled with purple loosestrife. Eva knows she could climb out here if she wanted, but something keeps her going. Maybe it's her obstinacy.

More likely, though, it's the thought of the look on Jennifer's face if she fails.

As she passes under the wide arches, the water lapping against the stone pillars, Eva feels her arms begin to get heavy and her fingers numb. It's cold in the shadow of the bridge and her heart pounds a steady rhythm against her wetsuit as she swims.

Under the bridge, the water is inky black, but when she emerges from its shadows she sees the river has turned to green now that the sun has come out.

It's quieter now, with most of the other swimmers having disappeared around a bend in the river. She's left her supporters behind at the start and won't see them again until she reaches the end of the race, where they'll be waiting with their home-made banners and smiles of congratulations.

Eva can see no-one ahead. How much further?

A wind ripples the surface of the water, making the reflections of the trees shiver. Her legs are heavy now and the band of her goggles feels tight against her temples.

She and Jennifer have always swum, first at the local pool and later for the local club. She's used to watching her sister hold up the cup, but she is aware

Illustration by Martin Baines.

that Jennifer's eyes never meet hers when a runner-up rosette is pinned to her swimsuit.

This race is different, though. It's about stamina; perseverance. She's used to swimming fast and her style is not suited to this distance. Why hadn't she trained more? Why is she doing this?

She knows the answer. It's because Jennifer wanted to, and ever since she could remember, Eva has wanted to be like her. Even now that she is old enough to know better.

The thrum of the outboard motor, when she hears it, is both a relief and a disappointment. The dinghy slows beside her. Pinned to the young man's jacket is a badge with the *River Arun Swim* logo on it. It bears his name – *Dan Ruthers.*

"Want a hand up?"

Eva shakes her head but she knows she's beaten.

"You look done in. Come on. I can see you've had enough."

Dan leans over and reaches out his fingers to her. He has a kind and sympathetic face. Has he guessed what it will cost her to reach up to take them?

She tries to pull herself up, but she's run out of strength and is glad when he helps her.

"I'm sorry." She sinks on to the seat opposite him, the water that drips from her wetsuit gathering in pools on the dinghy's floor.

"What for?" Dan hands her a towel.

"I'm not sure."

Pulling off her swimming hat and goggles, Eva towels her hair. All she wanted was to cross the finishing line with the other swimmers. To stand with a brightly patterned towel around her shoulders and feel the pat of people's hands in her back.

Most of all, she wanted to see her sister's nod of acknowledgement that she had done it.

"I didn't want to give up." She feels the tears prick at her eyes.

"You've swum two miles. You should be proud. It's a hard race to win."

"You don't understand. I didn't need to win. I just needed to finish."

Dan looks at her through narrowed eyes.

"It's that important, is it?"

She nods.

"She said I couldn't do it."

"Who?"

"My sister."

"And you believed her?"

He powers the dinghy forward and Eva watches the white wake it leaves behind.

"She was right."

Dan leans forward, one hand on the tiller.

"I have a brother. Two years younger. We fought like cat and dog when we were kids. He followed me around – proper little pest, he was."

They've rounded the bend and the swimmers are in sight. He raises his voice above the roar of the motor.

"I wasn't much good at school, but he was proper clever. When he got his degree, I was the one clapping the loudest."

"Really?"

"Of course. He was my little brother and I was proud of him."

They are catching everyone up. The man slows the engine and nods towards the water.

"Slip in here. No-one will ever know. You'll finish with the rest of them."

Eva does as he says, lowering herself into the water and feeling its coldness on her hands and chin.

It's not far from here to the finish line at the top of the lifeboat ramp and her short boat journey has given her back some strength.

Dan's right: no-one sees. They are too busy looking ahead to where the race will end.

* * * *

That was nearly 40 years ago.

Now, as Eva picks her way down the grassy bank with the others, feeling the wetsuit cling to her skin, she remembers the girl who had stood with the others on the concrete ramp.

She sees her shoulders draped in a towel and hears again the cheers of the crowd.

She remembers how her sister's face had broken into a smile when she saw her and the way she had pulled her into a hug, the cold skin of her cheek pressing against her own.

"I wasn't expecting that," she whispered.

Dan was right: Jennifer was proud of her that day. Maybe she always had been, but hadn't known how to show it. After all, how many teenagers want a little sister cramping their style?

But, despite everything, the satisfaction Eva had been expecting to feel hadn't come.

In her heart, she knew it was because she hadn't earned her sister's praise. She had no right to it.

Eva steps down into the water, shivering as the wind picks up. The river flows lazily away from her towards the distant sea. This time there is no race, just a web page full of sponsors.

You see, in the end it was Jennifer who hadn't made the distance. Her life had been a short race rather than a marathon, and she finally found a place where her sister couldn't follow.

Eva's strokes are measured, and she moves through the water slowly and steadily. She's older now and knows how to pace herself.

The river takes her under the cool arches of the bridge and around the bend, the other swimmers leaving her behind.

When she grows tired, she turns on to her back, sculling her arms and letting the river carry her downstream, the clouds ever-changing above her.

The thrum of an outboard motor breaks the tranquillity. When the dinghy slows beside Eva, she is both relieved and disappointed.

The man leans over the side. Pinned to his jacket is a badge with the *Swim For Life* logo on it. It bears his name – *Dan Ruthers*. He smiles at her.

"Want a hand up?"

She thinks of the promise she made to Jennifer, the money she'll raise to fight the dreadful disease that took her sister from her.

"No," she says. "I'm fine."

He already understands this, of course. In the years since they've been married he knows her almost as well as he knows himself.

He blows her a kiss and steers the boat away.

Eva swims on at her own pace, no longer a girl but a middle-aged woman in a wetsuit and a blue swimming cap. She imagines what Jennifer would think if she looked down on her.

Would she be surprised at the look of determination on her face? No, she thinks, probably not.

Jennifer would be proud of that woman. She knew she was. ■

Breakfast
In Bed

by Sandra Beswetherick

KAYLEE hopped down the stairs from one step to the next, singing.

"Happy Mother's Day to you! Happy Mother's Day to you!"

"Make sure you hang on to the rail," Charlotte cautioned as she followed behind carrying the breakfast tray loaded with empty dishes. "You don't want to slip."

"Your breakfast was good, wasn't it?"

"It was," Charlotte agreed with a wide smile.

Kaylee was their darling daughter. How fortunate she and Dennis had been that she'd come into their lives. How incredibly lucky to be entrusted with a six-week-old baby.

She'd been so perfect, yet so tiny Charlotte scarcely knew how to lift her sleeping form from the baby carrier. And now, at five, she was more beautiful than ever with her soft curls and dimpled cheeks. Charlotte felt her heart would burst with love.

"I stirred the pancake batter."

"I know. You told me."

They'd doted on her, of course, this longed-for child. She and Dennis wanted nothing but the best for her. For her to grow strong and independent; to be thoughtful and caring. To develop, as Dennis called it, a generosity of spirit.

"Can we make breakfast in bed again tomorrow?"

"Breakfasts in bed are mainly for Mother's Day. We could surprise your dad with one for Father's Day, though, if you like."

Breakfast in bed this time had gone better than she'd expected. No major spills on the bed sheets, and the blueberry pancakes had been delicious.

"Yes!" Kaylee cheered.

Dennis had tidied the kitchen after the two chefs finished preparing breakfast. Ingredients had been restored to appropriate shelves and the counter and cooker wiped clean. All Charlotte needed to do was wash their breakfast dishes.

She drew aside the curtains on the window above the sink and waggled the empty coffee pot at Dennis. He smiled and nodded.

"Once I finish with the dishes, we'll get dressed for our visit with Nanna

Illustration by iStock.

Morris." That was the reason Dennis was washing their car. "We're taking her to lunch this afternoon. For Mother's Day."

"Nanna Morris is Daddy's mum, isn't she? And Granny Collins is your mum." Kaylee had taken a great interest in mothers ever since Charlotte and Dennis had explained her adoption.

"We'll see Granny Collins later."

They wanted to be role models for Kaylee. To be examples of thoughtful and caring people. Charlotte smiled as she washed Dennis's coffee mug. Her loving husband seemed to be a natural, especially when it came to Mother's Day.

On her first Mother's Day she hadn't expected anything in recognition.

How Dennis had touched her heart when he'd given her a Mother's Day card with Kaylee's small handprint in pink and *I love you, Mummy* inscribed.

On her second Mother's Day, when Kaylee was beginning to walk, Dennis had given her a carnation and gently nudged her in Charlotte's direction. Kaylee, toddling towards her, flower firmly clenched in her chubby fist, her face a wide grin, could not have been more precious.

As soon as their daughter could help Dennis pour cereal into a bowl, the tradition of Mother's Day breakfast in bed had begun.

The coffee maker hissed and the aroma of freshly brewing coffee filled the kitchen.

Charlotte breathed deeply. Kaylee sat at the kitchen table, the tip of her tongue protruding from between her teeth as she concentrated on her paper and crayons.

Charlotte crossed the floor and stood at her shoulder, raising her hand to stroke her hair.

"What are you working on, love?"

"A Mother's Day card," Kaylee answered, not taking her eyes from her work. She was using another drawing, with which Dennis had helped, as a template. A big red heart with *I love you* on it, and lots of kisses and hugs.

"Another card for me? That's lovely."

"It isn't for you."

"Is it for Nanna Morris? Or Granny Collins?"

"No," her daughter replied, vigorously shaking her head. "It's for my other mummy you told me about. Mummy Judith. She needs a card, too."

Charlotte felt her heart wrench. To have to share her child's love with another woman was hard to accept.

"Do you know where she lives so we can send it?"

Charlotte took a deep breath for courage. How could she be less generous than her daughter?

"I know someone who does." The adoption agency would have Judith's address. "I'll make sure she gets it."

When Kaylee turned eighteen and wanted to meet her birth mother, could Charlotte be supportive? Could her thoughtfulness and caring match that of her daughter? What if Kaylee preferred Judith and loved her less?

"Mummy?"

"Yes, dear?" Charlotte knelt beside her daughter.

Kaylee handed her the card.

"It's for Judith, my other mummy." She clasped her hands behind Charlotte's neck and looked into her eyes. "You are my for-ever mummy, right?"

Daniel had explained their relationship to her in this way. For ever and always.

Charlotte's heart overflowed as she drew Kaylee to her.

"I am."

"That means lots of breakfasts in bed on Mother's Day, doesn't it?"

Charlotte laughed, still holding their daughter close.

"It does."

At that moment Dennis opened the outside door and encountered their little scene.

"What's this?" he asked, his eyebrows raised.

"Group hug," Charlotte answered, extending one arm towards him, knowing all would be well.

There would be love and caring enough for all, with a little laughter thrown in for good measure.

"In that case . . ." he began, as her little family was joined in a heartfelt embrace. ∎

Marilyn Monroe

Photoshot.

SCREEN goddess Marilyn Monroe was born Norma Jeane Mortenson in June 1926 and rose to the top in Hollywood, playing "dumb blonde" characters. It was a world away from her childhood upbringing, spending much of her time in foster care, as well as an orphanage.

It was her successful career as a pin-up model that was the springboard to her securing a few minor film roles, before signing a contract with Fox in 1951 and starring in comedies such as "Monkey Business" and "As Young As You Feel".

Her star image was sealed, however, with her roles in "Gentlemen Prefer Blondes" and "How To Marry A Millionaire". One of her biggest box office successes was "The Seven Year Itch".

But it was her relationships off-screen that were to make the headlines. Monroe had two high-profile marriages – to baseball player Joe DiMaggio and playwright Arthur Miller – but happiness seemed to elude the girl born in Los Angeles.

Having only really enjoyed fame for a decade before her untimely death, it's perhaps surprising that Monroe's icon status endures to this day. ■

Looking After Arlo

by Pauline Bradbury

W ELL, that is that," Molly told herself philosophically, giving a last wave to her fellow librarians as they locked up for the day.

The economic cuts had at last filtered down to their small library and as she had been the last in, she was the first out. She had loved sorting the books, tidying the shelves and helping to match book to borrower, so it was going to be a big hole to fill.

"Next week I'll start job hunting," she promised herself as she unlocked her car. "But for now I will have a nice weekend at Eve's."

By the time she had driven through the rush-hour traffic across town to the neighbourhood where she and Jake had lived before the accident that had taken him from her, her friend Eve had already left for her weekend away. Molly was very familiar with the key's hiding place and was soon inside the house being greeted by Sammy.

"You remember me, don't you?" she asked the tabby cat fondly. "We're old friends."

Such an old friend, Sammy seemed to be telling her as, tail in the air, he wound round her legs, that you must know where to find my supper!

"First things first." Molly smiled. "Let's get you sorted out."

*   *   *   *

The weekend passed almost too quickly. It was so nice to have a cat to fuss over again, and from a bedroom window she could peer over into her old garden. She was delighted to see that it was well looked after.

"I've really enjoyed it," she told Eve as she was stowing her overnight bag into the car on Monday afternoon. "Sammy is such good company."

"He's certainly the boss." Eve laughed.

Molly was about to get in the car when another old neighbour from across the road waved and hurried over.

"I was hoping to catch you," Sandra explained. "I know you've been looking after Eve's cat, and I was wondering if you would consider helping my mother

Illustration by Mandy Dixon.

out. She has to go into hospital for a check-up next week and the thought of her cats being on their own is worrying her more than the investigation."

Molly hesitated.

"Just for four days. Of course we would pay you," Sandra went on persuasively.

Molly was floundering. She adored cats and was only too ready to help people out, but she couldn't do it for money.

Before she could collect her thoughts, Eve broke in.

"What a good idea, Molly. You know you're going to be at a bit of a loose end now, and some recompense would be helpful. How much were you thinking of, Sandra?" Eve asked briskly, without embarrassment.

It was all decided before Molly could think of a good reason to decline, and she didn't know whether to be irritated or glad that she had been pressured into more cat-sitting.

"I suppose it could be fun," she muttered as she let herself into her flat later on, which seemed suddenly very quiet and empty. "I'm not comfortable about getting paid for it, though."

But even as she was thinking that, the beginnings of an idea flashed across her mind, and her heart gave an excited jump.

They had half promised to take her back at the library when one of her ex-colleagues retired in a couple of months, but she couldn't rely on that happening, so she would have to start looking at other options.

Why didn't she think about cat-sitting on a temporary basis? Done properly, of course, with references.

She could put an advert on the library noticeboard. Looking after other people's cats would make up for the fact that no pets were allowed in the tiny flat where she lived.

I'll still visit the job centre and apply for anything that's suitable, she thought, smiling to herself, but I'd better wait to see what happens at Sandra's mum's before I take the plunge.

*   *   *   *

As she parked outside the neat terraced house belonging to Sandra's mother the next week, she was feeling apprehensive. What if the cats lost their appetites without their doting owner? What if she couldn't get the cooker to work, or the heating?

If she was going to take this work seriously, however short-lived it turned out to be, she ought to make a preliminary visit to the house first. Mentally she chided herself and made a note of this for the future.

But her worries were needless. Sandra and her mother had left concise instructions, the house smelled of lavender polish, there were fresh flowers on the table and a pile of magazines by her bed.

And the cats! Two long-haired beauties, Bunty and Bella, tortoiseshell sisters who were as friendly and welcoming as the little house. They didn't lose their appetites and always curled up on the sofa with Molly for the evening's television.

It was a very happy four days, and even more so when Sandra brought her mother home again with the news that all was well.

"I can see my two babies have been well looked after, too." The old lady smiled thankfully. "Could I call on you again if I need to?"

"Of course," Molly replied automatically, and meant it.

I'll give it a go, she decided as she cooked her supper later.

*   *   *   *

After a visit to the job centre the next day, she called into the library with a neat handwritten notice for their board, advertising that cat-sitting could be undertaken by a competent lady at a reasonable fee, with references available.

"Well, that's done it," Molly whispered as she gazed at it. "Nothing ventured, nothing gained."

She bought a thick notebook and a large appointments diary, which she put by her phone.

"Dates, addresses, preliminary visit comments, after-stay comments, payments," she mused aloud. "I'm going to be really business-like about this."

But for the next three weeks the notebook lay untouched. There were no enquiries, let alone any bookings.

"Maybe not such a clever idea after all," she reported to Eve, who had been following events with great interest.

"Early days yet," Eve encouraged.

Nor was Molly lucky with the receptionist job for which she applied, though she hadn't been too hopeful about that. More disappointing was finding she was too late to apply for a sales job in a local high-street store which would have involved books and magazines. That would have been ideal.

Then everything happened at once. Three prospective clients rang on the same evening, all wanting cat-sitting fairly quickly but fortunately for different dates. With great daring Molly accepted them all.

"No backing out now," she remarked to Eve on the phone.

"Then go for it, Molly!" Eve urged enthusiastically.

* * * *

Several weeks later Molly sat at the table with her notebook, assessing the results of her first three cat-sitting jobs which she had been able to fit in alongside a temporary job she had found at her local newsagent.

She had kept meticulous details and now found herself with a little profit and a lot of pleasant experiences.

She glanced at her notes on each household.

Long weekend. Ginger tom called Buster. Happy-go-lucky family. Chaotic house but atmosphere jolly. Bed a bit lumpy, but would go again.

Midweek, four days. Professional lady. Elegant, minimalist house. Rather aloof Siamese called Ying Yang. Overpaid because so grateful. Very comfy bed. Would go again.

Two days only. Enchanting black kitten called Daisy. Doting young couple. House on large new estate. Put-you-up narrow bed, but would go again.

All very satisfactory, Molly thought, but what about the next one she had just accepted? This was to be in a village a few miles out of town.

She had agreed to do it because the caller sounded so nice, but then, just as she was about to ring off, the caller suddenly added that she was ringing on her brother's behalf, which had been a little disconcerting.

Going for a week's stay in a strange man's house was a bit daunting, but the caller had assured her that she herself would be there to let her in and settle her, and that a home help came in twice a week.

Molly waived the preliminary visit, especially as, for the last week of her temping at the newsagent, she had been asked to work full time.

As the village was not far away, Molly knew that she would easily be able to pop back to the flat to check on things if necessary.

"Though if I ever get any business further afield I shall have to be more practical and methodical in my planning," she told herself, enjoying the short trip out of town.

*   *   *   *

The house turned out to be a rambling old rectory, which was slightly alarming, but it was too late to back out, so she duly swung her car into the driveway.

With some trepidation she rang an old-fashioned doorbell, which she could hear echoing through the house.

A bit like a TV drama, she smiled to herself. Next I shall hear heavy steps and big bolts being drawn back, with probably a clanking chain as well!

Instead, light high-heeled footsteps hurried to the door, which swung open easily with no creaking or groaning, and a pleasant woman of about her own age stood there with a welcoming smile.

"Molly? I'm Fiona Milner. Do come in. It was such a relief to hear about your services from a friend of a friend. Usually I come and look after Arlo myself but I couldn't manage it this time."

As she was talking she led Molly through to the kitchen, where a gorgeous long-haired, black and white cat was sitting on the window-sill in a patch of sunshine.

Molly gave a gasp of admiration.

"He is so beautiful!" she said, and went over to stroke him. He started purring immediately.

"Yes, a winner of hearts." Fiona laughed. "My brother is dotty about him. He lives on his own, you see, so they keep each other company."

Molly had visions of a nice, white-haired old gentleman sitting in the evenings with Arlo on his lap, and perhaps a glass of sherry at his side.

"All your instructions are here." Fiona waved some typewritten notes at her. "I'll take you up to your room. I think Jean has put you in the Green Room. She's the home help," she added, seeing Molly looking puzzled.

"Yours is probably the tidiest room in the house," Fiona went on, showing her into a large, attractive room. "You'll see what I mean. Do feel free to explore. I'm sorry I have to dash, but Jean's mobile number is on the notes so she'll sort you out if you're anxious about anything. Nice to have met you."

And she was gone.

*   *   *   *

Molly soon understood what Fiona had meant. Apart from her bedroom and the kitchen, each room she peeped into had books everywhere: in boxes, on

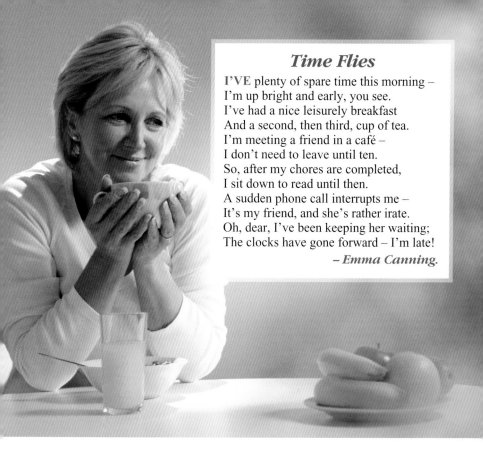

Time Flies

I'VE plenty of spare time this morning –
I'm up bright and early, you see.
I've had a nice leisurely breakfast
And a second, then third, cup of tea.
I'm meeting a friend in a café –
I don't need to leave until ten.
So, after my chores are completed,
I sit down to read until then.
A sudden phone call interrupts me –
It's my friend, and she's rather irate.
Oh, dear, I've been keeping her waiting;
The clocks have gone forward – I'm late!

– Emma Canning.

shelves, in piles on the floor, on window-sills and heaped on tables.

"Goodness." Molly was intrigued. "A library run riot."

She took one from the top of a pile.

"Jane Austen," she read, and perching on the arm of a chair was soon deep into the family life of the Bennet sisters until an aggrieved meow brought her back to her duties.

"I'm going to like it at your house, Arlo," she told him, laughing happily to herself.

She soon found that Arlo liked her being there, too, and would curl up beside her wherever she happened to be as she delved into one book after another.

"Have you seen the bedrooms?" Jean asked on one of her cleaning mornings. "Jam-packed, they are. Your bedroom was the same until I carted them all out."

"But where have they come from?" Molly hoped that wasn't being too inquisitive.

"Straight from Mr P's shop," Jean told her, vigorously shaking a duster out of the window.

"Shop?"

iStock.

39

"Yes. He had a second-hand bookshop. It was a sideline, like a hobby." Jean sounded slightly disapproving. "Then the rent went sky high so he hired a van and brought them all back here."

* * * *

After only a few days, Arlo seemed to think that Molly belonged to him. He accompanied her up to bed each evening and followed her around for much of the day.

"I do think you ought to be out in the fresh air more," Molly told him. "Let's go out together."

So it became a little ritual. While she walked round or sat reading on the garden bench, Arlo pottered about, too, and they always finished with a game of twig chasing.

Nearly a week later she was in the middle of dashing round the lawn, twigs and Arlo trailing behind, when somebody stepped out of the back door. And it wasn't Jean.

He was tall and thin with glasses, wearing skinny jeans and a rather startling red T-shirt emblazoned with the slogan *Books Are For Ever*.

"Hello, there," he called. "You must be Molly."

Molly came to an abrupt halt, her dishevelled hair falling across her face. She felt rather silly, as if she'd been caught out doing something childish. Also, she was acutely aware of her own T-shirt, which read *Keep Libraries Open*.

"Don't let me stop you." He smiled. "I can see that Arlo has found a good friend."

But then Arlo spied who it was and stalked over to greet his owner, curling round and round his legs and giving happy chirrups.

"I'm Toby Prince," he said, disentangling himself and holding out a hand. "And it seems we already have something in common." He gestured at their respective shirts.

"You're back early."

What a stupid thing to say, Molly admonished herself, but she was feeling confused because her imagined picture of Arlo's owner being an elderly gentleman was so different from this man not much older than herself, who had such a boyish grin.

"I hope you will find all is well," she went on stiffly, trying to be business-like.

"As long as Arlo is satisfied, then I am." He laughed. "But I must apologise for the untidy house. All those books."

"Books are fine by me!" Molly exclaimed. "I've loved looking through some of them. I guessed that would be all right as they seemed in no particular order."

"No," he acknowledged. "Just dumped straight from the van. How about a cup of coffee?" he suggested. "And if you're interested I'll explain why."

So Molly heard all about the second-hand book shop which he had run for years as a sideline to his professional job.

"I'm kind of a journalist," he explained. "Nothing glamorous. I report on scientific conferences and review scientific books. That sort of thing.

"Are you hungry?" he asked suddenly. "We could pop along to the pub for a toasted panini or something."

The next few hours went so quickly that they were back at the old rectory and Toby was filling the kettle for tea almost before Molly realised it.

She had enjoyed herself so much that she had filled him in about her personal life, about losing Jake so young and her work at the library. He had then confessed that a dramatic love affair in his twenties had made him cautious about long-term relationships.

"A crusty old bachelor, I am," he proclaimed, his kindly eyes twinkling, belying his words.

"I think I'd better pack my bag and get going." Molly drained her tea, suddenly feeling embarrassed about asking for her fee from somebody who seemed to have slotted into her life so easily in the space of a few hours.

"And I must pay my debts." Toby was stroking Arlo gently, but suddenly he caught Molly's eye, his eyes holding hers steadily.

"I was wondering . . ." he said. "As you enjoyed your library work so much, would you be willing to help me sort out my books? I've found a less expensive rental in town and intend to start up my shop again. I'm going to be away a lot over the next few months, so I'll be looking for somebody to run it for me."

His smile managed to be quizzical, teasing and warm all at the same time.

Molly didn't stop to think.

"That would be so interesting!" she told him enthusiastically. "I'd love that."

"Of course, it would all be done on a formal business footing," he went on. "Probably opening hours would be Tuesdays through Saturdays. I couldn't offer a brilliant wage, but it would be adequate. Though what about your cat-sitting?" he reminded her.

"If I only cat-sat at weekends it could probably all be fitted in," she told him cheerfully. "In any case, I only took it on to tide me over."

"We'll shake on it, then," he said, clasping her outstretched hand with both of his. "That's a deal. When can you come to sort it all out?

"Arlo would be happy if it could be soon," he persuaded teasingly, although something in his eyes told Molly that it wasn't only Arlo who would be pleased.

*   *   *   *

Molly smiled to herself as she arrived home.

What next, she wondered as she carefully recorded her latest job.

Seven days. Affectionate black and white moggy named Arlo. Handsome old rectory. Pretty bedroom. Books galore. Fascinating owner. Am definitely going again. ■

New Lanark, South Lanarkshire

DEEP in a gorge by the River Clyde in Lanarkshire, the village of New Lanark was established in 1785 for the manufacture of cotton. It was ideally suited for the mills whose water wheels were powered by the river. It became the biggest cotton mill in Scotland and traded all over the world, ceasing to make cotton only in 1968.

This success owed much to the philanthropist Robert Owen, whose far-sighted vision led him to develop the village along Utopian ideals. Owen thought that by treating his workers humanely, he could produce a society without crime, poverty or misery. To this end he built decent homes, provided free health care, an education system and even the world's first workplace nursery.

The systems he developed in New Lanark laid the foundations for other benevolent employers and for the worldwide Co-operative movement.

The site is now in the stewardship of the New Lanark Trust, which has restored the village and developed it into a Unesco World Heritage Site and award-winning visitor attraction. ■

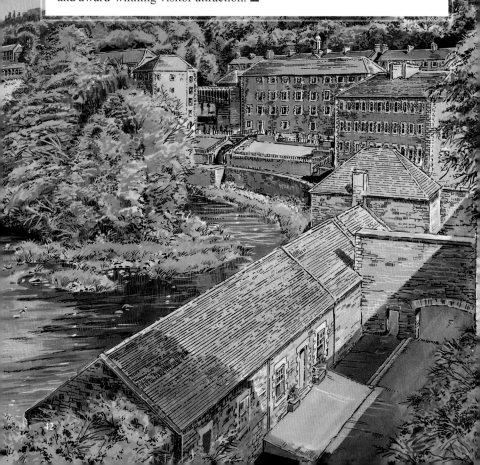

Illustration by David Young.

Lizzie's War

by Sandra Delf

L IZZIE turned the corner into London Street and was glad to see Tom riding towards her on his butcher's boy's bicycle. He screeched to a halt, dismounting clumsily. After recovering from this mishap, he walked gawkily beside her.

To Lizzie, Tom looked dapper in his flat cap worn on one side, ankle-length cuffed trousers and tweed jacket. A few years older than her, and the son of a farm worker, Tom had entered her life at Sunday school.

She had watched this friendly, mischievous boy from afar, but now he was beginning to notice her.

Happily bathed in the bright Easter sunshine of 1914, they had no idea of the troubles ahead.

"How are you today, Petal?" Tom asked.

He used Petal as a pet name for her, claiming she reminded him of the shy little flowers that peeped above the grass.

She smiled with embarrassment and glanced down at her feet, but didn't answer.

"Myself, I'm better for seeing you," he continued, leaning towards her, looking for a reaction.

Lizzie self-consciously smoothed down her beige cotton twill dress, its shapeless contours covering her slim frame. She was growing used to his flattery and enjoyed it, but was aware she wasn't the only girl who came in for attention from Tom.

"I've heard you say things like that to Emily King," she eventually replied. "And I don't know why you even talk to her. She's so standoffish."

"Of course she's standoffish. She's posh," Tom replied. "Posh people are like that."

"La-di-dah, you mean?"

"She may be la-di-dah, but that's because she's very clever. Look how good she is at teaching the young ones at Sunday school. She helps with the older ones, too. You should see the patience she has with my young brother, James, and nobody else can do anything with him. I think she should be a proper teacher. Anyway, she's always friendly to me."

Lizzie was taken aback by Tom's robust defence of Emily, but managed to smile through it. Tom was right, she thought. Emily was clever.

She fell silent.

Tom's playful mood was unaffected. He chuckled, leaned forward and, with his hands gripping the handlebars, manoeuvred the bike onwards in a high-spirited sprint.

"See you tonight at the Easter Dance, Petal," he called back.

Lizzie wished she had encouraged him more and hadn't let her jealousy of Emily get the better of her.

With her work at the greengrocer's shop finished, she scurried home along the back lane.

*　　*　　*　　*

That evening Lizzie arrived at the church hall in the best frock she owned: a flowered summer dress, not quite warm enough for the time of year.

She stood in the doorway for a moment, shivering and rubbing her arms to warm them up.

The room was bustling. She could just see the top of Tom's head across room.

As Lizzie moved further in, squeezing through the thick crowd, he waved her over.

"It's like Piccadilly Circus in here," he quipped, even though he had never been to Piccadilly Circus.

Last-minute adjustments were frantically being made to some seating. Bert Brown, the schoolmaster's son and newly appointed junior bank clerk, was in charge.

He frowned at Tom and issued instructions for him to find more chairs. Tom did Bert's bidding, then returned to Lizzie.

At that point Emily King breezed in and started making her way towards them. Tom fidgeted and tugged at his shirt cuffs. Lizzie watched a flush sweep over his face.

As Emily grew closer he stood tall and puffed out his chest. She looked him up and down.

"You're looking smart tonight, Tom," she said. "Pity your shirt isn't a little bit whiter, though."

Her eyes gleamed as she glanced at Bert Brown, her preferred beau, for approval.

Suppressing a smile, Bert turned away.

Tom, it seemed, was pleased Emily had even noticed him.

"Must try harder," he commented.

Lizzie thought it was a rude thing for her to say and couldn't understand why Tom was grinning.

Emily was dressed to the nines as usual, in a moss-green lace dress and with a large dark-green feather in her carefully arranged hair.

Lizzie was suddenly conscious of the greyish white collar of her own dress, and how faded its blue flowers were. Clothes were handed down in Lizzie's house.

But Emily didn't take Lizzie under her notice; she moved away with Bert to the other end of the hall. She didn't want Tom, Lizzie thought. She just likes his attention.

Lizzie enjoyed the rest of the evening, mostly in the company of Tom – apart from when Emily won a basket of brightly coloured eggs in the Easter raffle. How Lizzie would have loved just one of those eggs!

*　　*　　*　　*

By 1915 the recruiting sergeants had been working hard. Tom eagerly signed up and went to war.

"Take care of yourself, Tom," his father said briskly as they exchanged an awkward handshake.

Emily gave out white feathers, the traditional symbol of cowardice, to young men who didn't sign up immediately.

After being shamed by Emily with a white feather, Bert eventually enlisted and went to the Front.

The small provincial town steeled itself and set about supporting the war effort. The women put on a brave face but their eyes betrayed them. Normality had been taken for granted.

Lizzie had feelings of extreme fear and loneliness.

Easter brought Tom home on leave and to church on Sunday. He was standing at the back of the church when Lizzie entered.

She approached him, then hesitated, taken aback by his changed appearance. He was smart in his khaki, more upright, a little thinner, and there was aloofness in his eyes. His light brown mop of hair, which she was so fond of, was slicked back.

The church organ struck up, pounding out "Jesus Christ Is Risen Today". Lizzie retreated, slipping quietly into a nearby pew. Tom seemed even more out of reach than before.

At the end of the service, when Lizzie walked out through the arched doorway of the church, Tom was waiting outside, kicking at the gravel path. As she approached he jerkily extended his arm and handed her an envelope.

"For you, Petal," he said.

Lizzie opened it eagerly.

It was the nicest thing she had ever been given – an Easter card with a white border and an Easter bonnet on the front decorated with daisies.

At the bottom was an inscription – *With best Easter wishes* – and on the back he had written *Happy Easter, Petal*.

Lizzie was delighted and beamed up at Tom, but his expression didn't change.

At that moment Emily came out of the church. Tom called out to her. He took another envelope out of his pocket and gave it to her.

She opened it with a nonchalant air, glancing round in the direction of Bert Brown as she did so. Inside was a beautiful silk embroidered Easter card with a gold border.

Lizzie could just see the inscription, which contained a mispelling.

Best Easter wishes from your solider boy.

Emily gave Tom the sweetest of smiles then moved away towards Bert. Tom followed, listening intently to Bert's stories of his Army life.

Lizzie was crestfallen. Well, he's certainly not my solider boy, she thought.

She retreated from the churchyard, taking a short-cut home along the narrow dirt footpath by the allotments. When she reached the end she paused by the large chestnut tree.

Pulling off her hat, she flopped down on the dry grass and studied the precious card.

Despite being plainer than Emily's, she loved it . . .

*   *   *   *

The war dragged on. There was little news of Tom or Bert other than that they were on the battlefields of France.

Emily's patriotism grew and she became overzealous with her white feathers. She gave one to Tom's young brother, James, who was still under age. James felt the shame acutely, took off and signed up illegally before anyone could do anything to stop him.

His mother was distraught and made no secret of the fact that she blamed Emily.

With so many men having gone to war, Lizzie took on crippling work in the fields, learning to use ploughs and hoes. Her hands become rough and scarred but she felt she was "doing her bit". She was impatient for the end of the war and waited in dread that something would happen to Tom before it did.

Emily helped her father in the post office, where news of the war was often discussed. When lack of word of Tom became unbearable, Lizzie went to the post office and asked Emily if she had heard anything. She looked enviously at Emily's smooth hands and clean fingernails.

"There's been a report that Tom's missing," Emily replied curtly. "Not that it should make any difference to the likes of you, a member of the agricultural class," she added, with a withering glare.

Lizzie went cold. She was taken aback, firstly by the news that Tom was missing, but also at Emily's rudeness.

Clearly what had happened with James hadn't taught her to be more careful how she spoke to people, she thought. She might be clever and pretty, but she didn't always get things right.

Later, at home in her draughty bedroom, Lizzie took out the Easter card from Tom. She carefully unwrapped it from inside the frayed cotton handkerchief under her pillow.

Glad none of her four siblings were there, she slowly ran her fingers over it.

Frightened for him and missing him, she remembered how smart Tom had looked in his tweed jacket with its slight odour of Woodbine cigarettes. She was sure Tom would still be beyond her reach as a beau, even if Emily hadn't preferred Bert. But she wanted him safe home again and felt a deep longing for the wretched war to end.

The guns fell silent in November 1918. The war was over. But there was terrible news. Tom's young brother, James, wouldn't be coming home. He had been killed in action in France.

A few of his belongings had been sent home in a blood-stained handkerchief, bringing with them despair for his family.

The blame Tom's mother poured on Emily had a cooling effect on her confidence, and she stayed away from the family.

Lizzie steeled herself for more bad news, for Tom was still missing. Around her, for some there was jubilation and relief, but Lizzie felt only sadness for James and fear for Tom.

A month later, just after sundown, Lizzie's brother burst in through the back door into the tiny scullery.

"Lizzie, Tom's home!" George shouted. "He was seen walking down London Street."

Lizzie ran through from the front room, down the back opening and out on to the street before she hardly had time to think. After a few steps she stopped in her tracks.

She mustn't get so excited, she thought. There would be other people he'd want to see before her – his mother, father and, maybe, Emily.

She entered the house again by the back door, flew upstairs and fetched the Easter card she treasured so much. Then, after running back down the stairs and out into the street, she stood for a while leaning against the dirty red-brick wall.

How thankful I am he's home safely, she thought, clasping the card to her chest.

∗   ∗   ∗   ∗

She turned sharply at the sound of footsteps on the cobbles at the top of the street. Straining her eyes in the dim light, she could see a figure coming towards her.

The gas lights threw a shadow across his face, but she could see it was Tom, and that he was limping heavily. She expected him to say hello and walk on by, but he didn't. He stopped.

He had a large, ugly, jagged scar down one side of his face, but it was Tom. He really was back.

He smiled briefly and she noticed lines in his face that hadn't been there before. He stood awkwardly for a moment with his head bowed. He looked up and grinned and his eyes crinkled at the corners.

"I'm not the same handsome, cocky lad you used to know, am I, Petal?"

"You look fine to me, Tom. I'm just glad you made it back," Lizzie said. "I've been so worried. Have you been home and seen your family, and what about Emily? Have you seen Emily?"

"I've already been home, Lizzie. There's a lot of grieving for James, but relief to have me home. I don't think I'll go and see Emily. It's you I couldn't wait to see. Emily King always was a bit too la-di-dah for me. Anyway, clever people sometimes get things very wrong," he replied.

Lizzie's heart starting thumping. Slowly, Tom pulled a stained and crumpled envelope out of his pocket and handed it to her. It was another Easter card. *Happy Easter, Petal.*

"It's a bit scruffy. I've had in my pocket for a long time," he said.

"That doesn't bother me." Lizzie opened it and held it tightly, her face alight with joy.

"I always think of you at Easter, Lizzie," he went on. "Next year, if it's all right with you, can we spend it together and make it our best Easter ever?" ■

John Wayne

Photos

WITH his rugged good looks and slow drawl, John Wayne proved to be quick on the draw when it came to fronting cowboy movies such as "True Grit" and "The Shootist".

Born Marion Robert Morrison in May 1907, in Iowa, he was affectionately known as "Duke". He was certainly regarded as royalty when it came to movies, being among the top box-office draws for around three decades.

Did you know, however, that John Wayne worked tirelessly before reaching the heady heights of stardom? In fact, his first stint on a movie set was moving furniture around for filmmakers! He then progressed to being an extra, before finally cutting a break and getting his first starring role as the cowboy Breck Coleman in "The Big Trail" in 1930.

He featured in less well-known Westerns, even doing his own stunts, before landing a major part in "Stagecoach", which secured Wayne's place as a top actor. He then branched out into war movies, adding romantic comedies to his portfolio. But it was as US Marshal Rooster Cogburn in "True Grit" that he was to earn a Best Actor Oscar.

His final on-screen role, as J.B. Books in "The Shootist", is regarded by many as his greatest performance. ■

One Of Those Days!

by Annie Harris

C OME on, Olivia. Walkies!"
I rattled her lead enticingly, but the golden retriever just looked up
sleepily from her blanket.
"I know it's early, but some of us have got a job to go to, so stir
your stumps."

I showed her the lead again and she got to her feet. Giving me a reproachful
look, she ambled to the door of my flat. I was tempted just to take her for a quick
trip round the block, but I'd promised Jean, my landlady, that as one of Olivia's
paws was tender I'd give her a run on the grass in the nature reserve by the river.

Jean had rushed off the previous day to her daughter who was ill (I'd never
met her but she really did seem to make a habit of having her mother at her beck
and call). I'd been left in charge of the house, together with a long list of
instructions – and Olivia.

It was so early we had the reserve to ourselves, and it was lovely: the dew still
on the grass, birds flitting everywhere, and a couple of swans gliding
downstream on the river.

As I stood admiring them I gave Olivia her doggie treat and absently took a
bite of my muesli bar.

"Aaah! Ouch!"

I clutched my jaw as a sharp pain shot through one of my back teeth. When I
gingerly explored it with my tongue, I realised with a sinking heart that a large
filling had fallen out, taking with it what felt like half the tooth.

"Oh, no! I don't believe it!" I wailed, then winced again as a pounding ache
took over.

I couldn't stand a whole day like this, and besides, the rest of the dodgy tooth
might follow suit. I fumbled for my mobile, then realised it didn't hold my
dentist's number.

I hurried back to the car park with Olivia at my heels.

I put my hand in my fleece pocket for the car keys, but they weren't there. I
scrabbled frantically through all my pockets, but it was no use. I must have
fished them out along with the mobile.

Illustration by Mandy Dixon.

Nursing my mouth, I kicked my front tyre in temper, then dragged the bewildered Olivia back the way we'd come.

By the river, I forced down my rising panic and tried to stand exactly where my tooth had come to grief. Finally, just when I'd resigned myself to a mile-long walk back to the flat for my spare keys, then another mile back here, there they were, half hidden in a clump of dandelions!

I snatched them up and ran back to the car park with Olivia, having decided that all this was a new game, lolloping at my heels . . .

I skidded to a halt outside the house, right behind a decorator's van. Just letting himself in was a tall, fair-haired young man in overalls, carrying a stepladder.

I groaned again. I'd totally forgotten that among all the instructions left by Jean (anyone would think she'd be gone for six months rather than three days) was news that her nephew was coming to do some indoor painting. I had intended tidying up my little lounge before leaving for school.

He saw me coming.

"Hi, you must be Cassie, Auntie Jean's tenant. I'm Steve. Hello, lovely!"

This wasn't to me but to Olivia, who had thrown herself at him ecstatically.

"I thought you'd have gone to work before I got here." This was to me. "You're a teacher, aren't you?"

"Yes," I mumbled.

"I gather she's been summoned to Rachel's bedside. A right little prima donna, my cousin."

"Oh? I know Jean couldn't take Olivia because her daughter's allergic to dog hairs."

"Huh. So she says. She's trouble, that one. I remember the day I thumped her – purely by accident, of course – when she trashed my Lego farm!" He broke off. "Are you all right?"

"No. I've got terrible toothache – a broken tooth. I'm going to phone the dentist to see if I can get an emergency appointment, then I'll ring the head teacher to say I'll be late in."

"Well, I won't hold you up. I know what she wants done in her place, and it's just apricot emulsion in your shower room to brighten it up. Come on, Olivia. And good luck," he added sympathetically.

∗   ∗   ∗   ∗

Turning into the one-way street where the surgery was, I cruised down, desperately searching for a parking space, then saw one at the far end. The only problem was another car had pulled up, obviously about to reverse into it.

But my appointment was at eight-thirty – I had two minutes!

I shot into the space and was snatching up my bag when a hand banged on my window. I looked up to see a young man, scarlet with temper, scowling at me. Parking rage! Should I lock myself in? But he yanked open my door.

"That was a pretty low trick."

I looked ashamed.

"Sorry." I gave what I hoped was a winning smile. "I'm in an awful hurry."

"So am I. I just hope I can find somewhere else. OK, OK! Cool it!" This was not to me, fortunately, but to a driver behind us who was hooting his horn loudly.

He slammed the door, impatiently brushed down a head of dark curls which seemed to have been standing on end with fury, and stormed back to his own vehicle. It was a 4x4 estate, twice the size of my Mini, so he probably wouldn't have squeezed into the space anyway.

I thought of telling him so, but decided not to. Instead, I waited until he had moved off, then, hoping never to set eyes on him again, I hastily locked my car and ran indoors.

"Good morning." The receptionist smiled at me.

"Hello. Cassie Stone. You've fitted me in for an emergency appointment with Mr Spencer?"

"Ah, yes, of course. Broken tooth, isn't it?"

"Yes. Ouch!" I cried as another spasm shot through the molar.

"I'm afraid it won't be Mr Spencer; he's off with appendicitis. But Mark – Mr King – is fitting you in. He's our new partner."

I groaned inwardly. Richard Spencer had been my dentist for years. He and my teeth were old friends. He was kind and gentle, easing my way through all my dental tribulations which had been aided, no doubt, by my long love affair with liquorice toffees and sherbet lemons.

A Mr King, fresh out of college, no doubt, would have no time for cowards who practically needed anaesthetic for a clean and polish!

"Don't worry, dear." The receptionist must have sensed my apprehension. "You'll be in safe hands with Mr King. He's lovely. Just take a seat."

She clicked the intercom.

"Mark, your emergency is here."

A tinny voice squawked back then she turned to me.

"Go on in, dear. First door on the left. Good luck."

"Thank you." I gave her a sickly smile.

The dentist was washing his hands at the basin in the corner and spoke over his shoulder.

"Take a pew. Be with you in a moment."

Still drying his hands, he turned, and we stared at one another across the width of the surgery.

"Ah." His eyes narrowed. "The parking thief. We meet again."

I swallowed.

"Er, I'm sorry. Really I am. It was just that I was in such a hurry and I thought I was going to be late." I couldn't stop babbling. "And as I'd been fitted in, I . . ."

"All right." He held up his hand. "Truce. Now, into the chair with you."

I lay back and he sat in his swivel chair beside me.

"Don't look so terrified. I don't intend getting my revenge by yanking out all your teeth."

As he pulled up his face mask, I thought I glimpsed a twinkle in his eyes.

"Now, let's see the damage. Open wide. Hmm, nasty. Does that hurt?"

"Yes," I whimpered, and closed my eyes.

✳   ✳   ✳   ✳

"There you are, Cassie!" Sarah, our headmistress, smiled sympathetically as I popped my head round the office door. "All right?"

I grimaced.

"I need a crown. He's put a temporary one in for the time being. Still, at least it's stopped hurting."

As I hurried along the corridor, I couldn't hear a sound from my six-year-olds, which was strange for they tended to play up with Alison, my classroom helper.

Still, all to the good. I certainly didn't feel like a difficult day with them, and boy, they could be difficult – sorry, lively – when the mood took them!

I opened the classroom door and was greeted by 20 woebegone faces – 21 if you included Alison.

"Good morning, children," I said breezily. "Have you been good for Mrs Weaver? I'm sure you have."

"Miss Stone." Alison came across to me. "I hope the dentist sorted you out."

"Yes, I –"

"Good, good." But I knew she wasn't really listening. "The thing is, Cassie," she whispered, "it's Frisbee."

"Frisbee!"

I stared past her to the red cage, the dwelling place of our resident hamster.

Personally, I thought it a daft idea having a hamster as the classroom pet, because they spend daylight hours cosily curled up in their nest of shredded toilet paper, only emerging when the children are home, asleep. But I'd inherited him when I took over the class and dared not serve him with an eviction order.

"He seems to be, well, not too good." Alison was still whispering.

With a sinking heart, I walked across to the cage and looked down. Dear little Frisbee was lying on his back, all four pink paws in the air.

"Perhaps he's asleep," I said, in a falsely jolly voice.

"No, he isn't, miss." One of the boys sniffled. "He's dead."

A girl sobbed and soon all 20 six-year-olds – plus Alison – were in tears.

I felt like joining them, putting my head down on my desk and howling with misery!

Steve's van was still parked outside when I got home, and I groaned inwardly. What a day!

At least poor Frisbee's demise had created opportunities for classwork. I had intended removing his cage during break, then disposing of the tiny corpse while the children were having their lunch, but one bright spark demanded that we "give him a real funeral, miss, and we can all write a poem to read."

This was greeted with such enthusiasm that I agreed and it was really very touching to see them chewing their pencils as they composed their eulogies. Three of the toughest boys spent their break carefully making and decorating a cardboard coffin.

They decided that he should be buried over by the clump of shrubs in the far corner of the playground, so I got Bill, our caretaker, to dig a nice hole there.

After lunch we all solemnly gathered round and every poem was recited, some of which brought tears to my eyes, and Frisbee was solemnly interred.

*　　*　　*　　*

I gathered up my schoolwork and let myself into the house.

"It's only me," I called.

"Oh, hi, Cassie." Steve appeared in the hallway, looking harassed and clutching a dishrag.

"What's happened?" I asked as I took in the splodges of apricot all over his overalls. "Have you finished my shower room? Don't worry if –"

My voice tailed off. Yes, one wall was finished and looked lovely. But the floor and the rest of the cubicle was awash with paint.

"Oh, no!"

How many times had I said that since I'd got out of bed this morning?

"I'd hoped to get it cleared up before you got back." And indeed there were signs of frantic scrubbing.

"How did it happen?"

"You know you put Olivia out in the garden before you left?"

"Yes."

"Well, I'm afraid you didn't. Or rather, you did, but you can't have quite closed the back door. I was on the stepladder when Olivia appeared. She must have nudged the door open. First thing I knew, she threw herself at me, I dropped the tin and fell off the steps! So it's all Olivia's fault."

"No, it's mine," I said ruefully. "What with my toothache and being in a rush, I must have left the door off the catch."

I surveyed the wreckage. Should I just lie down on the floor and never get up again?

"Did you hurt yourself?" I asked belatedly.

"No, I'm fine, thanks."

"And where's Olivia now?"

"Back outside in disgrace, covered in apricot spots."

I started laughing; weak, hysterical laughter.

"Sorry." I gasped. "It's just, if you knew the day I've had . . . Parking rage, dentist's chair, funeral . . ."

"Funeral?"

"Don't ask. Look, don't worry about this. I'll clean it up."

"Well, if you're sure, thanks. I'll get off to the shop before they close, buy some more paint and pop back tomorrow to finish the job."

As soon as Steve had gone I made myself a cup of tea then set to work, finally letting Olivia skulk back indoors and sponging the spots off her coat so she no longer resembled an apricot Dalmatian.

When it was all at last done, I realised I was hungry. What to have?

With the tip of my tongue, I explored around my tooth. The gum was still quite tender from the injection I'd needed so the dentist could probe around it.

I'd closed my eyes when I saw the needle approaching but I'd hardly felt it. Even so, he'd warned me to be careful until the permanent crown was in place.

After his initial jokiness, Mark King really had been very gentle, with genuine sympathy in those grey eyes.

So much so that, when he said he'd need to see me again in 10 days' time, I realised that, for the first time ever, I was actually looking forward to a session in the dentist's chair!

Anyway, tonight it had better be soup. The problem was, I had no soup in the cupboards . . .

∗ ∗ ∗ ∗

As I wheeled my trolley into the supermarket I thought I might as well complete a terrible day and do my week's shopping two nights early. I stocked up with tomato soup (sometimes only tomato soup will do), and everything else I could think of, then steered my trolley towards the nearest checkout.

As the woman ahead of me in the queue unloaded enough to feed a small army, I saw that another checkout was about to open. I made for it as fast as my trolley would move and was almost there when, out of the corner of my eye, I saw another trolley come speeding down the aisle.

No-one, I determined, was going to beat me. I thrust my trolley forward and the two collided with a loud clang. I scowled round at my rival – and groaned. Parking rage this morning, trolley rage at teatime!

"Ah. We meet again, Miss Stone. How's the tooth?"

"As you see." I gestured towards the pile of three-for-two tins of soup. "Actually, it's not bad, thank you."

"Good.' He gestured to the till. "Be my guest. Your need is greater than mine."

"Thank you."

And we actually exchanged a smile. A real smile, not a teeth-bared sort of smile.

I was still packing my stuff away in the boot of the Mini when he appeared.

"You look tired," he remarked, helping me load my bags.

"It's been quite a day. My tooth, paint everywhere, Frisbee –"

"Frisbee?" He raised dark brows in enquiry.

"It's a long story," I said wearily.

"Tell you what, I've had a heck of a day, too – you were my easiest patient, by far – and I'm just off to the Old Mill. They do really good curries on a Wednesday. You look much too tired to be opening tins of soup, so can I tempt you? A mild curry would be fine for you, I promise."

His eyes really were a lovely shade of grey. I'd thought that even when they were frowning in concentration in the surgery, and now they were smiling down at me.

"Thank you. I'd like that, Mr King."

"Great. Oh, and if it's a date, it's Mark."

That's how, from being one of those days, that evening turned into something much, much nicer, sitting at the riverside, listening to the gentle splashing of water on the restored wheel.

Oh, and the vegetable and coriander curry, which didn't hurt my tooth at all, was very nice as well. ∎

Johnstown Castle, Wexford

THE call of peacocks punctuates the calm of the beautiful surroundings of Johnstown Castle Gardens, near Wexford in the Republic of Ireland. Visitors picnicking in the grounds frequently encounter the birds roaming around the lush ornamental gardens surrounding the 19th-century castle.

The estate was established in the 12th century by the Esmonde family, originally from Norman France, then confiscated during Cromwell's time before being acquired by the Grogan family in 1692. They remained in the castle until 1945 and oversaw the development of the ornamental gardens by the Kilkenny architect Daniel Robertson between 1844 and 1851.

In 1945 the castle and grounds were presented as a gift to the Irish nation, and the property is now under the care of Teagasc, the Agricultural and Food Development Authority.

Though the castle isn't open to the public, the grounds and gardens remain a popular visitor attraction, as is the neighbouring Irish Agricultural Museum, on the site of the old farm. ■

57

Tiny Steps

by Enid Reece

I T was all about Charlie and tiny steps.

Allan sat on the park bench watching Jinny walk towards the café alongside the duck pond. The chill of autumn was in the air and she'd decided a cup of coffee was in order.

Shoving his hands in his pockets, he grinned to himself. His wife was nervous of today's outcome and he wasn't surprised. He was a little nervous himself, but it was all going to work out.

He glanced over at the pond. A couple of children were at the edge with their mother, who dipped her fingers into a paper bag and handed each child some seeds.

Years flashed back as he remembered doing the same with Graham, his excited chatter as a family of ducks snatched at the food before paddling away, then returning for a refill.

He should be doing this with Charlie. He should be doing a lot of things with his grandson.

Jinny emerged from the café, two paper cups in her hands, careful not to slop them as she negotiated the steps.

She stopped to watch the children, a wistful look on her face. She missed Charlie as much as Allan did.

"What time is it?" she asked as she handed him a cup.

"About ten minutes after the last time you asked," Allan teased, taking a sip.

"Sorry. What if –"

"No what ifs," he interrupted. "Let's keep calm and it will happen. Tiny steps, remember?"

He reached out and squeezed her hand. There were shadows under her eyes. He wanted to stroke them away, to take the worry and throw it in the nearest bin.

She gave him a smile that didn't reach her eyes.

"You and your tiny steps."

He grinned.

"They usually work, don't they?"

Allan had been cautious by nature since childhood, from deciding what he wanted for Christmas to the friends he made.

Even courting Jinny had been one small step at a time, from admiring her on the bus as they both rode to work, to the note he'd given her as she stepped off, a stop before his.

Illustration by Jim Dewar.

He smiled, recalling the first smile she'd given him as she clasped the note in her hand.

Jinny was fidgeting again. Allan reached out and gave her hand a reassuring squeeze.

"Not long now, love."

They both stared ahead, lost in their own memories.

"I'll just put these in the bin," she said, draining her own cup and reaching out for his.

He watched her walk towards the bin and prayed that all would go well today.

"Do you think he'll still recognise us?" Jinny asked as she sat back down on the bench. "It's been three years and he was so young the last time he saw us. He'll be seven soon. Almost grown up."

Allan reached out and clasped her hand again.

"We sent the pictures as a reminder."

"The ones we took that last weekend. What a wonderful time we had."

Allan remembered. Graham and Kirsty had been busy finishing the packing and decided that it would be a good idea for Jinny and Allan to take Charlie for the long weekend.

The weather was good, no clouds in the sky and no wind in the air, so they decided to go to the beach for the day. A bucket and spade was purchased at the seafront shop, Charlie demanding that they should build the largest sandcastle on the beach.

They succeeded, too. Charlie and his grandad took turns filling a bucket full of sand, and the shape of an impressive castle began to form. A moat was called for and Charlie shouted in delight as a circle of water surrounded it.

Allan bought a red plastic windmill which he planted on top of the castle. A breeze caught the sails and Charlie clapped his hands as he watched the windmill spinning. It was such a special time.

"He'll still think we're strangers," Jinny said, pulling Allan back to the present. "Do you remember when Graham and Kirsty first met? They were so happy. The whirlwind romance; the wedding within six months; Charlie's arrival. Then it all went wrong."

Allan squeezed her hand.

"Some people aren't as lucky as us. Marriages go wrong – it happens."

"But grandparents shouldn't suffer."

"Sometimes things happen that we can't control, love."

Allan recalled the excitement in Graham's voice when he'd revealed the job offer he'd received.

"It's an opportunity of a lifetime, Dad," he'd said. "Just think, all that sunshine. Charlie will love it."

The only drawback was that it was in Australia. Allan and Jinny were upset about the long distance, but tried not to show it. How could they when Graham was so excited?

So, with a positive attitude, they waved off their son and his family with plenty of promises of Skyping and the occasional visit.

All went well for the first 12 months. Then Kirsty became homesick, and the arguments began. Graham insisted on staying; she wanted to return home. Within months Kirsty and Charlie flew home without him, the marriage in tatters.

Graham and Jinny, eager to see Charlie, attempted to arrange visits, but Kirsty always made excuses. It never seemed to be convenient. Then Kirsty moved house and all contact was lost.

That had been three years ago. Charlie was growing up fast and his grandparents were missing it all.

"What a blessing that you bumped into her mum last month," Jinny said, her focus still on the pathway.

It was, Allan thought, remembering the meeting and the first tiny steps. It turned out that Kirsty was back in town. A few phone calls along the way and she'd expressed her regret that Charlie had no contact with his grandparents.

Country Cottages

THE names of country cottages
Never fail to please,
Each attracting my attention
When I find ones like these:
"Candlestick" or "Custard Pot",
"Cherry Tree" or "Rose";
Each has some connection
To names that someone chose;
That favourite flower or memory
That's fixed to wall or door,
A perpetual reminder
Of what that name was for.
"Bumblebee" will beckon me,
"Mousehole", "Cosy Cott."
Each remembered, loved and known,
Like sweet "Forget-me-not".
A cottage white-washed, painted,
It may be thatched or stone,
But each name reads – translated –
That word we know as "home".

– Dawn Lawrence.

There were even plans for Charlie to visit Graham in Australia, something Allan knew his son was looking forward to. Being estranged from his son was not easy.

"I really miss him, Dad. I should have made more of an effort to see him, but my money only stretches so far and plane tickets aren't cheap. We Skype, but it's not been the same," Graham had said during his last phone call.

"You've done the best you can, son."

"Have I, Dad?" Graham asked, regret sounding in his voice. "I felt sure our marriage would work. Maybe I should never have suggested we emigrate. Perhaps we would still be together now."

"Things have a way of following a path, Graham. Don't tear yourself apart over what might have been."

"At least Kirsty and I are communicating better now, and to be honest I'm happy that she's settled back home."

"Yes, you should be grateful for that. Nothing worse than battling parents."

Graham gave a laugh.

"I can't remember you and Mum ever having a row."

"Oh, we've had a few," Allan replied with a smile. "Only we did our best not

iStock.

to argue in front of you. We made sure of that."

"Anyway I can't wait to see him, take him to the park and teach him to play cricket. You know I wanted him to come over before, but Kirsty felt he was too young," Graham went on. "He's older now and really excited about flying on his own."

"Are you sure that's safe?" Allan asked.

"It's fine, Dad." Graham assured him. "Kirsty has arranged it all with the airline. She explained the situation and they have stewards to look after children who travel on their own."

"How about Mum and I travel with him? We could make a holiday of it for all of us. We've been planning to come anyway."

"That would be great, Dad. I've missed you and Mum as much as I've missed Charlie. Talk it over with Kirsty when you meet up."

*   *   *   *

"They're here," Jinny said now, bringing Allan back to the present.

He watched as Kirsty stood at the entrance to the pathway. Beside her was Charlie. He'd grown so much. Allan felt the loss of the missing years, but now wasn't the time for regrets.

He watched as Kirsty bent down and spoke to Charlie, then gave him a gentle nudge forward.

Allan reached out for Jinny's hand as Charlie walked towards them. Their grandson. Cautious at first, then with recognition, his feet began to move faster until he was running towards them.

"Grandad! Grandma!" he shouted, running into Jinny's arms.

Allan looked towards Kirsty to give her a nod of thanks for leaving them to get reacquainted with their grandson. He looked down at Jinny. Charlie was still clasped in her arms and he wiped away a tear of joy at seeing them together.

He cleared his throat and pulled out a bag from his pocket.

"Goodness, how you've grown. How about we all go and feed the ducks? Not too old for that, are you?"

Charlie shook his head and reached for the bag.

"See you later, Mum!" he called over his shoulder.

"We'll meet you in the café if that's OK?" Allan said, looking at Kirsty.

She smiled.

"I'm so sorry," she apologised. "I was angry. I know now that I shouldn't have taken it out on you. Or Graham, for that matter."

"Let's move forward, not backwards. Tiny steps."

Kirsty gave him a tentative smile.

"I'd like that. I'll meet you in the café."

Allan reached out and squeezed her shoulder before moving towards his wife and grandson. This time he took a giant step. ■

Illustration by Mandy Dixon.

Meeting Matilda

by Teresa Ashby

ARE you all right, Chrissie?" I asked the older woman who sat opposite me at work. "Is it your dad?"

She looked lost as she put the phone down and stared at it.

"My dad? No, it's my daughter. Lottie's gone into labour."

"What was that?" Rob, our supervisor, looked up. "It's too soon, surely."

"I know," Chrissie replied, biting hard on her lip. "I promised I'd be with her, but she's two hundred miles away and I'd booked time off around her due date. I don't know what to do."

"Go," Rob said. "Right now. You can be there in a few hours. Your daughter needs you, Chrissie."

"I can't just leave," Chrissie replied. "And what about my dad?"

I looked round the office hoping someone would speak up, but no-one did.
"I'll go round and see him," I heard myself say. "I can make sure he's OK and get anything he needs."

"Oh, would you, Fran?" Chrissie seemed to crumple with relief. "I arranged for my cousin to stay with Dad when the baby was born, but she's away on holiday just now."

I was already regretting it. I hadn't worked there long and I kept myself to myself. I'd never been very good at making friends and I felt horribly out of my depth in this big office.

Chrissie started gathering things up and was in such a state she knocked her coffee cup off her desk and must have dropped her keys about three times.

"You can't drive, Chrissie," I told her, sticking my neck out again as I looked imploringly at Rob. "She can't drive, Rob."

"Fran's right," he agreed, and he took hold of her shoulders and looked deep into her eyes. "There's no way I'm letting you drive all that way in this state."

"I'm not in a state," she protested as she dropped her bag and the contents spilled all over the floor.

"I'll drive you," he said. "And I'll stay with you. No arguments! The department will manage fine without us, won't you?"

We all agreed. Even if we had to work extra hours, we'd do it. Everyone loved Chrissie and we all knew her daughter had lost her last baby when she was born too early.

She stopped for a moment and looked around the office.

"I don't know what to say," she whispered.

"Say goodbye," Rob told her, then ushered her out of the door.

I was so glad he was going with her. Rob was strong in a quiet sort of way. He was the rock Chrissie needed.

I had no idea what was wrong with her dad, but he never left the house and he was very dependent on her.

"Good luck with Chrissie's dad," Barbara said as we headed to our cars that evening.

I hoped I wouldn't need it, but something I did need was Chrissie's address, so I asked Barbara.

"It's a bungalow in Buttercup Lane," Barbara said. "All I know is it has a yellow front door."

When I arrived in Buttercup Lane, I found two bungalows with yellow front doors. One front garden was full of stone animals dressed in little suits. A toad and a badger each pushed a wheelbarrow out of which spilled red and blue flowers.

The other front garden had been gravelled and had two flower pots under the front window with a small clump of marigolds in each.

Surely Chrissie's garden would be the no-frills one like Chrissie herself, so I headed towards it.

I tapped on the front door and moved the handle. It opened up into a gloomy hallway.

"Mr Hedges? It's Fran from work."

Chrissie had texted me to say she'd told her dad to expect me.

The doors into the hall were open, but no light came from the rooms as all the curtains were closed. I wished I'd never volunteered for this.

I was halfway down the hall when I heard a low, rumbling growl.

"Mrs Whiskers?" I said, but surely it couldn't be a cat growling like that. From what Chrissie had said, her dad's old tabby chased off any dogs that dared set foot in their front garden.

"She hides behind one of the wheelbarrow pots with her bottom wiggling, then leaps out," she told us at work. "The poor dogs don't know what's hit them."

My heart began to pound.

Wheelbarrow pots? I was in the wrong bungalow.

The dog appeared in the doorway of the bedroom nearest the front door. It was huge. Not just tall, but heavily built with a head the size of a Halloween pumpkin.

"It's all right," I said, edging towards the back of the bungalow and hopefully another door. "Good boy."

He took a few steps towards me, issuing a series of low woofs.

"I'm just leaving," I said.

The dog lunged at me. I swear he took off and flew through the air. I tried to run, but tripped over my own feet and ended up sprawling flat on my face with the huge, slobbering beast standing over me.

I squeezed my eyes tight shut.

Oh, why hadn't I just minded my own business? Someone else would have looked in on Chrissie's dad, I was sure. I should have stayed in the safety of my shell where I belonged.

But what I was facing here was nothing compared to what Chrissie's daughter was going through. She was only about 30 weeks into her pregnancy, which was ten weeks too soon.

I pretended to be dead when I felt the dog's big wet nose snuffling round my neck, then he huffed hot breath in my ear and if I hadn't been so terrified, I'd have laughed.

I only had myself to blame for this. I was an intruder in the dog's home and he was just doing his job. Normally I got along better with dogs than people, but it seemed I couldn't even be friends with a dog any more.

Suddenly his hot, wet tongue sloshed down the side of my face and I heard his tail hitting the radiator as he wagged it.

I opened my eyes slowly and saw a large shiny tag in the shape of a bone hanging from his collar. In the dim light I saw his name. *Matilda.*

"Matilda?" I said, and her ears tried to stand up, but just stuck out sideways as her whole bottom wiggled from side to side. You'd have thought I was her long-lost best friend. "Good girl!"

Suddenly the hall was flooded with light as the front door opened and a worried voice called out.

"Is that you, Fran? Did you fall?"

"I'm fine," I said, getting to my feet while Matilda bounded down the hall to greet the voice's owner. "How do you know who I am?"

"I saw your car," he said. "I was concerned when you didn't appear. Chrissie said you were a bit shy. I'm Bill, Chrissie's dad. Where's Elise?"

"I don't know. I've only seen Matilda."

"Elise!" he called out. "Where are you, love?"

I must admit he didn't seem frail or helpless as he searched the bungalow. Then he found Elise, still in bed.

"She's conscious but very weak," he said. "I'll stay with her while I wait for the ambulance. Could you take Matilda along to my bungalow? She can stay with me until Elise is better."

*   *   *   *

He came back to his bungalow once Elise had been taken to hospital.

"Are you all right?" I asked.

"Never better," he said. "I haven't gone further than the garden for almost two years. And now I'm going to take Matilda for a walk." He looked a little uncertain. "At least that's the plan."

"Would you mind if I tagged along?" I said.

"That would be great." He looked relieved.

I don't know what had got into me as I was useless at making conversation. I needn't have worried, as Bill talked enough for both of us.

"I wouldn't say I was agoraphobic," he said. "But pretty close. I lost all my confidence after my wife died and it was easier to stay at home than go out and face the world. I still feel uneasy, but it's so long since I even tried to leave the garden, it's not surprising."

His mobile phone rang and he stopped to answer it.

"That was Chrissie," he said when he'd finished. "They've given Lottie something that will help the baby's lungs mature if it is delivered early. Poor Chrissie. She'll be so worried. I should be there with her."

"Rob will look after her," I said.

"Rob?"

"From work. He insisted on driving her."

A slow smile spread over Bill's face.

"Did he now?" he said. "That's interesting."

"Is it?"

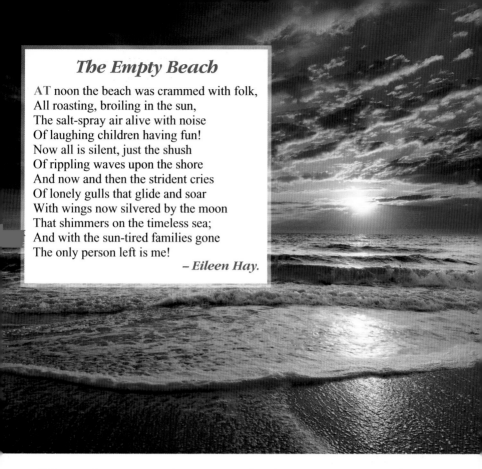

The Empty Beach

AT noon the beach was crammed with folk,
All roasting, broiling in the sun,
The salt-spray air alive with noise
Of laughing children having fun!
Now all is silent, just the shush
Of rippling waves upon the shore
And now and then the strident cries
Of lonely gulls that glide and soar
With wings now silvered by the moon
That shimmers on the timeless sea;
And with the sun-tired families gone
The only person left is me!

– Eileen Hay.

"They used to go out together years ago when they were teenagers. He always looked out for her, did Rob." He looked wistful. "I'm sure he still has feelings for her, and if she'd only let herself, she would for him. Sadly, after her divorce, she's sworn off romance. Anyway, how about you, Fran? How are you settling in?"

"Oh, you know," I said with a shrug.

I realised I had a lot in common with Bill. If I didn't have to go to work, I would have stayed at home in my flat rather than face the world.

I'd moved to a different town and a different job, trying to leave my past behind, but it haunted me still.

I wasn't exactly jilted at the altar, but it was close. I could easily see how someone could fall into the trap of hiding away.

I called in on Bill on my way to work in the morning. He was just back from taking Matilda for a walk.

"I'm going to visit Elise at the hospital," he told me. "When she comes home, you'll have to meet her. After all, if it wasn't for you going into the wrong

iStock.

bungalow, I wouldn't have known she was ill."

When I got to work, everyone wanted to know if there was any news from Chrissie.

Every day I popped in to see Bill and Matilda, and eventually Elise when she came home from hospital, fully recovered. Somewhere along the way I'd found my old self and looked forward to company instead of dreading it.

Some of the people from my department invited me out for a drink one night after work and, instead of making my excuses and scurrying home, I went along with them and had a great time.

None of this would have happened if I'd stayed quiet the day Chrissie got the phone call from her son-in-law. I would have stayed in my sad, lonely shell and I would have never got to know all these lovely people.

*　　*　　*　　*

Exactly nine days after Chrissie left, I was out walking Matilda with Bill and Elise one breezy evening. The wind was blowing through the trees and Matilda was lolloping along, enjoying every minute.

Elise was holding Bill's arm and he was smiling as if he'd won the lottery. I was smiling myself, too.

Bill's phone rang and he listened for a moment then punched the air.

"I'm a great-grandad!" He whooped. "Finlay William was born an hour ago, weighing a whopping four pounds two ounces, which the midwife said was a wonderful weight for thirty-two weeks."

I could hear Chrissie's excited voice, but not what she was saying.

"Mother and baby are doing fine," he added. Then he went quiet for a moment and looked at Elise, then at me.

"Yes, I'm out," he said with a smile. "We're down the lane with Matilda."

His hand was shaking when the call ended and he slipped the phone back in his pocket.

"Well, that's a turn-up," he murmured, looking pleased. "You're a bit of a miracle worker on the quiet, Fran."

"Me? I haven't done anything."

He reached for Elise's hand and they exchanged knowing smiles.

"I think you've done more than you realise," Bill said. "Chrissie said if it wasn't for you, Rob wouldn't have had the courage to suggest driving her, and they wouldn't have fallen for each other all over again."

"And if it wasn't for you, Bill would never have left his front garden and come to my rescue," Elise added, giving Bill's hand a squeeze.

I couldn't stop smiling as we carried on down the lane with Matilda, for Chrissie and Rob, for Bill and Elise, and for the safe arrival of the new baby. I was even smiling a little bit for me.

I'd come out of my shell at last and it felt great. ▪

Rita Hayworth

Photoshot.

BORN Margarita Carmen Cansino in October 1918, Rita Hayworth was raised in Brooklyn, New York.

A highly successful actress who notched up more than 60 films in her career, she was also a great dancer and was adept in ballet, tap, ballroom, and Spanish routines. Fred Astaire, with whom she made two films, even called her his favourite dance partner.

Hayworth's parents both danced and her father wanted her to become a professional dancer, while her mother hoped she would become an actress – so she fulfilled both their wishes!

In her early career, Rita was often cast in an exotic foreign role, until she took on her mother's maiden name and changed her hair colour to red – the changes certainly seemed to open more doors for her.

She starred in "Only Angels Have Wings" with Cary Grant and Jean Armour, and it proved a box-office hit. It also confirmed Hayworth as a bright new star and made her a pin-up girl for military servicemen.

James Cagney shared the billing with her in another box-office hit, "The Strawberry Blonde", and she immediately became one of Hollywood's hottest actresses.

One of her greatest successes was the 1944 movie "Cover Girl", which also starred Gene Kelly.

In all, Hayworth's career spanned 37 years. ∎

Marsha's Clear Out

by Jacqui Cooper

GOODNESS, Janey, when I gave you that sofa I didn't think you'd let the dog sleep on it!"

Janey had spotted Buster on the sofa at the exact same moment Marsha had.

"Basket!" she ordered the dog, but of course he ignored her.

"He's not usually allowed on it," she apologised to her mother-in-law, hustling him off the expensive piece of furniture which until recently had graced Marsha's sitting-room.

"I'm not criticising, Janey. It's just that it needs specialist cleaning."

"I know," Janey replied. "It was very good of you to give it to us. I'll try to take better care of it."

But with a husband, three boisterous kids, a dog, a cat and a full-time job, Janey couldn't help thinking longingly of the sofa with washable covers she'd picked out before Marsha made her generous offer.

Janey was late leaving work next day and she still had to stop off at the supermarket to grab something for tea. Then she had to take Sara to Brownies and Liam to Cubs.

She was harassed and late and already apologising that it was fish fingers for tea again, when she hurried into the house to be met by the delicious aroma of lasagne and the sight of Ben and the kids seated at the table while Marsha lifted a bubbling dish out of the oven.

"Janey!' Marsha said warmly. "Perfect timing."

Janey dumped her carrier bags by the door.

"Hello, Marsha. I didn't know you were coming round."

She looked quizzically at Ben, who gave a tiny shrug, indicating that he hadn't known, either.

"I know how busy you are so I thought I'd surprise you," Marsha replied. "I hope that's OK?"

"Of course it's OK," Ben said, piling food on to his plate. "Mum's lasagne is the best. Far better than fish fingers, eh, love?" he asked Janey.

Janey nodded. Secretly, however, she was thinking that, while a surprise was nice, it would have been even nicer if someone had thought to call and spare her

Illustration by Helen Welsh.

the unnecessary trip to the supermarket.

Quickly she pushed that ungrateful thought aside.

"Your mother is driving me crazy!" she said to Ben later when the kids were in bed and Marsha had gone home. "She makes me feel completely inadequate."

"Don't be silly. She likes helping, that's all. I think she's lonely."

"Lonely?"

Marsha was always so busy that Janey hadn't considered that.

But it could explain her coming round so much, especially recently. Marsha had retired last year from her teaching post and Janey supposed she hadn't yet adjusted to having so much free time on her hands, especially since many of her friends still worked.

She made a mental note to help Marsha make some new friends and improve her social life. Then, maybe, Janey wouldn't feel under so much pressure to live up to Marsha's high standards.

*   *   *   *

Next day Janey phoned Marsha to thank her for the lasagne.

"I can give you the recipe," Marsha said eagerly. "It isn't difficult, as long as you use fresh ingredients and cook it long and slow. So much better than out of a jar."

Like Janey always made? She gritted her teeth, knowing Marsha didn't mean any offence.

"That would be wonderful."

She was working out how to casually mention the knitting circle she had found at the community centre when Marsha got in first.

"Actually, Janey, I'm glad you phoned. There's something I've been wanting to discuss with you . . ."

The dog flew past with a toy action figure in his mouth. A child raced after him, yelling loudly.

"Buster!" Janey yelled. "Liam, be careful! Oh, for goodness' sake. Sorry, Marsha. Here, talk to Ben while I sort this out."

"Ben? No, I'd rather –"

But Janey thrust the phone at Ben and hurried off to restore order.

When Janey finally finished for the evening, she flopped down on the sofa beside Ben.

"What did your mum want?"

"To give us that fancy coffee machine."

"She did?" Janey was surprised. "I got the impression she had something she wanted to say."

"Like what?"

"I don't know. She just sounded odd. And why is she giving us the coffee machine?"

She looked around the sitting-room. As well as the sofa, they also had Marsha's coffee table and her fireside rug.

"In fact, why is she getting rid of everything?"

"Dunno." Ben wasn't even a little bit curious. "She says she's having a clear-out and wants it to go to a good home."

People having a clear-out kept the best stuff and got rid of the rubbish. Marsha was doing the opposite.

*   *   *   *

Janey was still pondering this the next day when, while driving through town, she spotted Marsha coming out of the estate agents. The traffic was heavy and by the time she managed to turn and go back, there was no sign of her mother-in-law.

When Marsha popped round that evening, Janey waited in vain for her to say something.

"I saw you in town today," Janey ventured finally.

"Oh?"

Did Marsha look cagey?

"Everything OK?" Janey asked.

Marsha took a deep breath.

"Actually, Janey –"

The phone rang. Janey ignored it, waiting for Marsha to finish, but Marsha

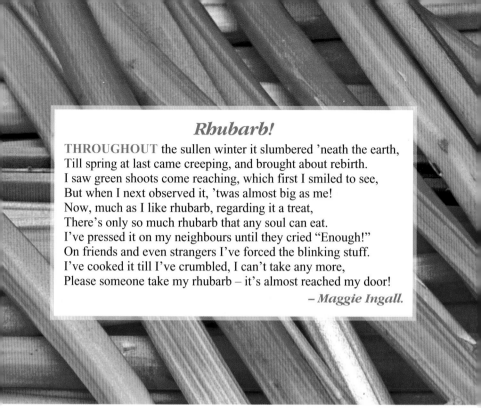

Rhubarb!

THROUGHOUT the sullen winter it slumbered 'neath the earth,
Till spring at last came creeping, and brought about rebirth.
I saw green shoots come reaching, which first I smiled to see,
But when I next observed it, 'twas almost big as me!
Now, much as I like rhubarb, regarding it a treat,
There's only so much rhubarb that any soul can eat.
I've pressed it on my neighbours until they cried "Enough!"
On friends and even strangers I've forced the blinking stuff.
I've cooked it till I've crumbled, I can't take any more,
Please someone take my rhubarb – it's almost reached my door!

– Maggie Ingall.

seemed to change her mind.

"I was just doing a few errands. Why don't you take that call?"

No mention of the estate agent.

Janey grabbed Ben after Marsha had gone home.

"Your mum is selling the house!"

"No way!"

Janey told him what she had seen.

"Where is she moving to?" he demanded.

Janey glanced around the room, which was beginning to look more like Marsha's sitting-room than theirs.

A worrying thought occurred to her.

"You don't think she's hoping to move in here, do you?"

Ben shrugged.

"It makes sense, I suppose. The house could be getting too much for her. It would be nice having her here to cook for us, and great having her iron my shirts. I mean," he amended quickly, seeing Janey's face, "she'd be company for you."

Janey didn't need company. What she needed was to be able to relax in her own home, even if the dishes weren't done straight away or the lunches made.

iStock.

There was no way could she do that with Marsha here.

As much as she loved her mother-in-law, the thought of living under the same roof as her was terrifying.

But how could she say that to Ben? Or Marsha?

*　　*　　*　　*

Janey redoubled her efforts to find some new interests for Marsha.

Armed with a list, she picked up the phone. Of course, some subtlety was called for.

"Hi, Marsha. I'm thinking of joining a book club. How would you like to come with me?"

Marsha didn't like the book club. Or the sewing club. The ramblers were too muddy and the photographers too technical.

Janey was running out of ideas. Marsha still hadn't broached the subject of moving in, but Janey lived on tenterhooks waiting for it to come up.

As the days passed, she watched in growing despair as Marsha continued to empty her house into theirs.

"Do you think I should put a profile on a dating site?" she asked Ben in desperation.

"I thought you liked me," he replied amiably.

"For Marsha, silly."

He looked shocked.

"Fixing up my mother? Don't you dare. At least not without her permission."

Janey had a rare day off midweek. After Ben had gone to work and the kids were off to school, she sat down with a cup of tea and a magazine: a rare treat for her.

Then Marsha popped her head round the door.

She glanced round the kitchen, sticky with the remains of breakfast.

"Is this a bad time?"

Janey valiantly ignored the mess.

"Of course not. Tea?"

"Don't disturb yourself," Marsha said. "Here, I brought you this."

She produced a beautiful enamelled biscuit tin and placed it on the counter.

"There, that brightens the place up, doesn't it?"

She noticed a dribble of honey on the table and reached for a cloth.

"You can sit down, Marsha," Janey said. "You don't need to clean."

Marsha looked in surprise at the cloth in her hand.

"Sorry. Habit. I can't abide a mess."

She seemed completely unaware of what she'd said.

In fact, she looked nervous, and in that moment Janey felt utterly selfish.

"Have a seat, Marsha," she said gently. "Tell me what's up."

Marsha sat.

"There is something I want to talk to you about."

"Maybe we should wait for Ben?" Janey tried.

"No. It's you that will be more affected. I need to discuss it with you first."

Janey braced herself.

"Oh, dear, this is very difficult."

Never a truer word!

"Let me make it easier for you," Janey said. "I saw you at the estate agent. I think I know what you are going to say."

Marsha wasn't listening.

"Really quite awkward . . ."

"It's OK, Marsha. We'll manage."

"I'm leaving!" Marsha blurted out. "I know I should have told you sooner, but I just didn't know how."

Janey stared. That was not what she had expected to hear.

"Leaving? Where are you going?"

"India."

"What?"

"Oh, I'm not handling this very well. Do you remember Patricia, the headmistress from my old school?"

Janey did remember Patricia, an energetic woman who had retired a few years ago. She nodded.

"We kept in touch," Marsha said. "She's working for –" She named a large charity which was a household name. "Patricia runs a small village school in India. She adores the work and says the children are wonderful, but she's so busy. They need more staff."

"And you're going?"

"Yes." Marsha nodded eagerly. "For a year, initially. I'll rent my house out, which is why I'm giving you all my nice stuff. I wouldn't want to leave it for someone to treat carelessly. This is something I've always wanted to do but I never had the nerve. Patricia being there just makes it easier."

"Marsha, that's wonderful news!" Janey said, and meant every word. "But I don't understand why you thought I'd be so against it."

"Well, I know how much you rely on me, Janey, what with the housework and the children and you working full time. And Ben isn't much help. But I hadn't realised till recently just how lonely you were. I feel guilty and selfish going off like this."

"Lonely?" Janey was mystified.

"All those groups you asked me to join with you. To be honest, Janey, I think you stretch yourself too thin. What's the expression they use today? I think you need to chill."

Janey jumped to her feet and hugged Marsha.

"You're right. I will definitely do my best to chill. My very, very best!" ■

Glen Turret, Perthshire

AMID the glorious Perthshire countryside, Glen Turret, north of Crieff, offers beautiful, peaceful moorland scenery at the foot of the Highlands.

The area is a favourite with walkers and wildlife enthusiasts. It's home not only to the grouse for which the glen is famous, but also to more elusive residents such as the golden eagle and the Scottish mountain hare. Smaller than the brown hares to be found in the Lowlands, the coat of the mountain hare turns from brown in summer to white in the winter. There are quite a few of them living here, so you may be lucky and spot one!

After all that walking, you might feel in need of a little warmth to restore you. A visit to nearby Glenturret Distillery and the Famous Grouse Experience should do the trick. One of the oldest distilleries in Scotland, the popular tour tells the story of how water from Loch Turret and Ben Chonzie has been transformed into the "water of life" or *uisge-beatha* (whisky) since at least the early 18th century. ■

Illustration by Jim Dewar.

Catch Of The Day

by Diane Wordsworth

THE fishing season was about to start again and the Belshaw family found it the main topic of conversation at breakfast.

"I suppose that means we'll be fending for ourselves again at the weekend," daughter Sarah joked.

"No more lifts on Saturdays to cricket," Harry, the elder of the two boys, teased. "And we have an important game this weekend, too."

"Don't worry, son." Peter harrumphed. "I'll be there to cheer you on."

Only the youngest, Davey, seemed truly happy at the prospect.

"Leave Mum alone!" he defended. "She does enough for all of us the rest of the week. She's entitled to a day off."

77

"But every week?" Peter complained. "It's most weeks from now until next March."

"That's right!" Sarah agreed, enjoying the light-hearted family banter. "Honestly, Mum, you can be so selfish!"

"Selfish?" Jenny said. "I'm here every day of the week cooking, cleaning, mending and washing clothes. The beds don't make themselves and, last time I looked, we didn't have a Hoover fairy."

She knew they were all only teasing, but it still narked her a little that they couldn't be more supportive.

"Not one of you ever chips in to help. You leave everything to good old Muggins."

"But you are here all the time," Harry reasoned. "You don't have anything else to do."

He winked at his dad.

"And fishing's meant to be a man's game, anyway."

"Yes," Sarah agreed. "It's so embarrassing having a mother who goes fishing. I have to tell my friends you're meeting Great-aunt Dora in Timbuktu for the day."

"And they believe that?" Jenny asked.

"Well, I think it's cool," Davey said quietly. "And I can't wait until I can go, too."

"You'll never get your wheelchair down the bank!" Harry teased.

"Harry!" both of his parents admonished at the exact same time.

"I was only kidding."

Harry ruffled his brother's hair, but Davey didn't seem that bothered as he tucked into toast and Marmite.

"The kids might have a point, Jen," Peter said finally. "I mean, can we really afford it this year?"

"Number one," Jenny replied, ticking the item off on her index finger. "It's the only thing I do for myself. The only thing! Number two." She ticked her middle finger. "It costs twenty-five pounds, if that. I think you'll find that most other wives are considerably more high maintenance than that."

"But we're saving up to take Davey to America for his operation."

Hmm, maybe her husband had a point.

But it was only one day a week.

"Perhaps you'd prefer it if I went to the hairdresser every week instead of washing it myself. Perhaps you'd prefer it if I needed the latest fashions to wear at the school gate. Perhaps you'd prefer it if I liked a bottle of wine every night.

"I don't drink, I don't smoke, I don't dye my hair, I don't require a Chelsea tractor in which to do the weekly shopping. I fish. And I look after you lot."

Sarah opened her mouth to speak but was silenced by another fierce glare from her mother.

"One more word from any of you and I'm off to live with Great-aunt Dora in Timbuktu!"

And the family burst into a fit of giggles until she chucked a cushion at them.

*   *   *   *

The opening of the new fishing season was greeted with a massive three-day festival and competition sponsored by one of the biggest local tackle manufacturers. First prize was a 16-metre pole worth more than £3,500.

Jenny sighed. She would love a brand-new pole of her own for a change, instead of using second-hand or borrowed all of the time, but she knew she could never afford one, and she didn't often win a match.

Never mind, she'd enjoy the day sitting on the riverbank, watching the water, battling wits with the fish. None of the family had ever come to encourage her, but they would only be a distraction. Even little Davey. She preferred it that way, as did many of her angling chums.

The klaxon went, marking the start of the contest, and silence descended along the banks of the river. The exhibition ground behind the anglers buzzed softly with visitors, but that was more like white noise for the men and women fishing, and was quite calming, actually.

Jenny caught a little roach very early on and popped him into her keep net. In a competition like this one, on a river where weights weren't generally great, every tiddler counted. Several more followed.

As the sky clouded over and fat drops of rain began to fall, news trickled along the bank that a pike was stealing fish while anglers were reeling them in. Jenny hoped that someone would catch the pike before it reached her.

They weren't allowed to keep the pike if they caught it, but pike usually lost interest anyway once they had been caught and went to skulk in the shallows in shock for a while.

A journalist bobbed along the bank, too, homing in on the more famous anglers for a quick word and a short snap. He didn't recognise Jenny's name on her board but he did hesitate for a while.

Jenny concentrated on the water, staring ahead, but as she reeled in another slightly bigger fish she heard the shutter go on the journalist's camera and smiled to herself. He'd just bagged himself a bit of a novelty. But Jenny knew he'd see other female anglers further down the bank, some of whom had even been on telly.

She was still chuckling quietly to herself when she realised she was actually doing quite well. Probably about ten pounds or so – not bad for a river, and not bad for a woman. The pike must have given her a wide berth.

The river darkened and swelled under the purple cloudy sky and some of the

fair-weather anglers started to pack up.

"How have you done?" Jenny asked one of her neighbours.

He shook his head.

"Not very well. I've not caught anywhere near as many as you," he replied, packing away some of his gear. "I'll try again tomorrow."

Jenny would have liked to come back the next day, too, but she'd had her weekly fun. She was content.

As she reeled in her first big catch of the day another of the early finishers paused in pushing his trolley to watch her. When the small carp was safely netted, he spoke.

"You've caught more than me in just that one fish."

"Really?" The fish only weighed about four pounds and was just one of her haul. Maybe, just maybe . . . but she couldn't allow herself to hope.

Not yet.

✳   ✳   ✳   ✳

The finishing klaxon sounded and three teams of lads with scales made their way along the riverbank. They weighed Jenny's catch. Fourteen pounds.

iStock.

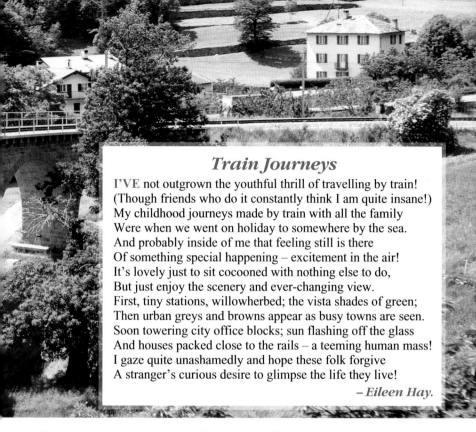

Train Journeys

I'VE not outgrown the youthful thrill of travelling by train!
(Though friends who do it constantly think I am quite insane!)
My childhood journeys made by train with all the family
Were when we went on holiday to somewhere by the sea.
And probably inside of me that feeling still is there
Of something special happening – excitement in the air!
It's lovely just to sit cocooned with nothing else to do,
But just enjoy the scenery and ever-changing view.
First, tiny stations, willowherbed; the vista shades of green;
Then urban greys and browns appear as busy towns are seen.
Soon towering city office blocks; sun flashing off the glass
And houses packed close to the rails – a teeming human mass!
I gaze quite unashamedly and hope these folk forgive
A stranger's curious desire to glimpse the life they live!

– Eileen Hay.

That was a good weight, she realised, especially when it won her the section and then the women's catch of the day.

But when it beat the men's results, too, she was delighted. And she'd won that brand-new pole!

At the awards ceremony the runners-up in all categories accepted tackle and cheques for their prizes.

When it came to Jenny's turn she was asked if she wanted the pole or the cash equivalent.

What a quandary!

It didn't take her long to make up her mind. There was no contest.

"I'll take the cash, please," she said, only a little disappointed at not getting the pole.

As she told the journalist, £3,500 would go a long way to paying for Davey's trip to America.

*   *   *   *

Back home, Peter was overjoyed.

"See?" he said to the children. "I told you all we should let your mum enjoy her little hobby." He grinned, giving his wife a hug.

Jenny just smiled. She hadn't told them how she'd opted for a cash prize instead of a pole.

Sarah chucked a cushion at her dad, but Harry tackled him to the floor while Davey giggled his head off.

"We're going back to the festival with her tomorrow, too," Peter announced when he came up for air. "As a family."

$$* \quad * \quad * \quad *$$

The next morning the Belshaw family returned to the riverbank, sticking to the paths for the most part to accommodate Davey's motorised wheelchair.

They played hook-a-duck at one of the stalls, Harry won Sarah a giant teddy bear at the shooting range and they ate hotdogs and pancakes.

"It's Jenny, isn't it?" a voice behind them said. "Jenny Belshaw?"

Jenny spun round to see Tim Avery, owner of the tackle company which was sponsoring the three-day event.

"Yes," she said.

"Congratulations on your win yesterday."

"Thank you."

"I would have liked to have chatted with you but you dashed off in such a hurry."

"Yes. My family were expecting me home," she explained, sweeping her arm to demonstrate them.

"We understand. And this is Davey, your youngest?"

"Er, yes. How did you know?"

"That journalist told me your story after you'd dashed off."

"Oh." Jenny wasn't really sure what else to say.

Tim cleared his throat noisily.

"The thing is, Jenny, we were wondering . . . That is, if it's all the same to you, we want to give you another prize. We'd like you to accept a fishing pole as well as the cash."

"Oh! I couldn't, really –"

"Of course you can! It's not the same as yesterday's – we raffled that one off in the end. But if you'd like to accept a different model? It's not as valuable, but it's still worth almost two thousand pounds."

He waited expectantly, but Jenny's mouth opened and closed several times with nothing coming out.

She looked rather like the fish she caught.

And so it was her husband who replied on her behalf.

"She'd like to accept, thank you very much."

"Splendid," Avery said.

And they all shook hands and followed him to the tackle tent. ∎

Paul Newman

Photoshot.

B **ORN** Paul Leonard Newman in January 1925, in Ohio, Newman was a Hollywood hunk who enjoyed one of the most enduring film careers.

This multi-award winning actor wowed audiences with his powerful performances in the likes of "The Hustler", "Cool Hand Luke" and "Butch Cassidy And The Sundance Kid". Twenty-five years after "The Hustler", Newman reprised his role of Fast Eddie Felson in "The Color Of Money" in 1986, which won him an Academy Award.

Newman is up there with all the legends of the big screen and he also managed to find personal happiness, too, enjoying one of the most enduring marriages of the film greats. He and actress Joanne Woodward were cast together in "The Long, Hot Summer" in 1957 and married a year later. They celebrated their golden anniversary just months before Newman's death in 2008.

Not only was he truly one of the greats of the big screen, also directing movies, but he also managed to find time to steer a course as a professional racing driver, as well as being an entrepreneur and giving generously to charities. ∎

Magical Dreams

by Rebecca Mansell

NANA TESSA, please tell us the story. Mummy won't mind."
"Please, Nana Tessa, we love to hear it, and we aren't tired."
I smiled at my two little cherubs with their rosy cheeks and big
blue eyes fringed with dark, long eyelashes. Identical twins; it
was just about impossible to tell them apart.

They peered at me so beseechingly, with their rainbow-coloured duvets pulled
right up to their small chins.

I adored my grandchildren and always looked forward to seeing them during
my daughter's weekly visit. Carol needed a break sometimes so I would take
Katie and Sophie on countryside walks and help them with their homework. Try
to, at least – things had changed since I'd been at school.

As for "my story", even though I'd told it to them frequently, their excitement
never diminished at hearing it. I wasn't so sure it was an appropriate bedtime
story, really.

Long after I'd left their bedroom after telling it, I would hear them talking
animatedly to one another, and the following day they always looked a little
bleary eyed when they smiled at me and said, "Good morning, Nana Tessa" at
exactly the same time.

But then, long ago, I'd also stayed awake at night. Though what had stopped
me sleeping had been rather different . . .

I settled into the chair opposite my grandchildren, pulled a cushion on to my
lap and smiled.

"When I was your age, I wanted a bicycle. A nice red one. It seemed as if all
my friends had one."

"We both have bikes." Katie beamed. "But we are very lucky."

"Hush!" Sophie nudged her. "Let Nana Tessa tell her story."

I chuckled softly and continued.

"I loved my grandpa very much, but he never used to give me presents at
Christmas or my birthday. Just a card. My mother told me that it was because
Grandpa went without when he was a child, as he had to look after his brothers
and sisters, and that he was trying to teach me a valuable lesson. I was too young

Illustration by Philip Crabb.

to understand. All I could think about was getting a bicycle.

"We lived in a little village and I had a paper round. As I had to deliver to the houses in the neighbouring villages as well as our own, I thought it would be much easier if I had a bicycle."

"And more fun!" Sophie giggled. "Oops, sorry, Nana Tessa."

"Grandpa suggested that I just walk faster." I smiled as I continued. "He said I could learn a lot from reading the newspaper, too."

I hugged the cushion to my chest as I reminisced.

"I did read it, but I found it to be quite boring, really. Mostly it was news about fêtes and committee meetings and the occasional story about the local town building more houses. As a child, I didn't think it was interesting and preferred my Enid Blyton novels."

"We haven't read Enid Blyton, have we, Sophie?"

"No. Mum said she will get us the school series, though," Sophie said, a little crossly. "Please carry on, Nana Tessa."

"Then Grandpa gave me a pen for my birthday and I was very surprised because, like I said, he never gave me presents. I think it was because he thought I was old enough to write. Well, of course, I had been writing at school, but Grandpa seemed to believe that I needed to write something that I had created myself.

"At the time, I hadn't written proper stories yet. At school, we only had to write about what we had done during the school holidays and draw a picture, but I had never made up a story. I didn't really think I had the imagination, to be honest. Then, that Christmas, Grandpa gave me a big notebook. My mother instructed me to write a story and show it to Grandpa. She said he would like that."

"And he did like it, didn't he?" Katie couldn't help but interrupt, her eyes bright. "He liked the animals in your story."

"Yes, he did." I smiled. "I was inspired by the books I had read, and because I loved animals I decided to write about a magical wood, with talking badgers and squirrels that helped a lost little boy find his way home."

"Do you still have it?" Sophie asked eagerly.

I thought for a moment.

"I think I gave it to your mother. You will have to ask her."

"Go on, Nana Tessa." Katie sat up in bed, pulling her teddy bear close. "What happened next?"

"Well, Grandpa read all my stories," I continued. "I suddenly found I had a hobby. I really enjoyed writing, especially as my tales delighted Grandpa so much. He encouraged me and gave me ideas for new stories."

$$* \quad * \quad * \quad *$$

I paused as I reflected, the memories of years gone by warming my heart.

"One day," I said to my enraptured audience, "he visited us and came into my little bedroom to give me something."

"I know what he gave you!" Katie said excitedly.

"Be quiet. You're getting mixed up with the ending." Sophie frowned.

"No, I'm not," Katie replied indignantly. "He gave you his book, didn't he, Nana Tessa?"

"The book he wrote himself," Sophie said quickly, before her sister could say another word.

"Yes. Girls, you know the story so well! He did indeed give me his book. It was a book full of short stories that he had written over the years, and it was very good."

I laughed.

"His writing was hard to understand in parts, but his tales were also about animals and creatures from the moon. He wrote about a young man who travelled into space with a monkey."

Both girls burst out laughing. They always did at this part.

"So I made a decision. I saved up all my money from the newspaper round and bought a very old typewriter from my employers. They had one that they didn't use any more and it didn't cost very much, but it still took me many weeks to save for it."

"And then . . . ." I paused for dramatic effect, enjoying the animated expressions on my grandchildren's faces. "I typed up all his stories! I did it at night when everyone was asleep because I didn't have time during the day, what with school, my homework and my paper round."

"Didn't Great-nana ever hear you?" Katie asked curiously. "Mummy always knows when we aren't in bed."

"Luckily for me, my mother never heard me. My bedroom was at the far end of the house and she always slept soundly. In fact, she could sleep through a thunderstorm! I was always very tired, though."

I shook my head.

"It took me a long time to type up all of my grandpa's stories. Gradually, though, I got faster and faster on that old typewriter. Of course, I was still writing stories, too, otherwise Grandpa would have been suspicious. Then, at long last, it was done."

"How many stories did you type?" Sophie asked, even though she knew the answer.

"One hundred stories," I answered. "Some were quite long, too."

"When you gave your grandpa his stories, what did he do?"

Both girls were sitting up in bed now, watching me intently, their eyes shining. This was their favourite part of the story.

"Well, he danced!" I laughed. "I'd never seen him with so much energy. He just picked me up in his arms and we danced around the room. He was delighted to see his work looking so professional. Like a book, he said. He told me he would cherish it for ever.

"And it was then that I realised that I didn't want a red bicycle after all. At least, not at that time."

"You wanted to write!" Sophie and Katie said in unison.

"Well, yes, but it was more than that. I suppose what I really began to appreciate was that giving felt better than receiving. My grandpa's response to what I had done gave me even more incentive to write.

"So that's what I did. I continued to show him every story I wrote and he said they were getting better and better. That was when I realised just how much I loved writing. It was more than a hobby."

I gazed at my two little cherubs and their captivated expressions. This next part of the story always made me feel sad.

"My parents took me round to see my grandpa. He wanted to speak to me and it was very important. He told me that one day he wouldn't be with us any more and he wanted me to have something. He said he would leave it to me in his will and that it would affect my future."

I smiled gently at my girls.

"I was upset. I didn't want to talk about it, and in my mind he had already given me something very precious."

"Your love of writing," Sophie said wisely.

"Yes," I agreed. "By this point, I simply had to write. I felt like I was delivering a message to the world in my stories."

"But the day did come when Grandpa left us. By this time I was a teenager and I was so sad at losing him that I forgot what he had said about his will."

Sophie and Katie were solemnly watching me as I felt the familiar lump rise in my throat. After all these years I still missed my grandpa.

"When my parents told me that he'd left me a book in his will, I wasn't surprised. After all, he was always telling me to read more so that I could write even better."

"But the book was very old, wasn't it, Nana Tessa?" Katie said softly.

I smiled.

"Yes. It was an antique and very rare. Inside the book, he'd left me a note."

I could still remember the words that were shakily printed in capitals on a small piece of paper.

Take this book, sell this book (and this you must) to set your dreams free and those of your own grandchildren.

"I had no idea he had such a book. I think he kept it especially for me. It was all he had that was valuable."

"So you sold it . . ." Sophie began.

"And you went to university," Katie finished.

I laughed.

"Well, you know what happened after that."

"You became the best writer in the world!"

"I don't know about in the world . . ." I protested.

"It's true," Sophie said seriously. "Everyone has heard of Tessa Hartley. You are famous, and so are we because we're your grandchildren!"

I chuckled.

"Well, you both are my best fans."

"What was the name of the book your grandpa told you to sell for you to go to university?" Katie suddenly asked.

I glanced up, surprised. In all the years I had been telling my grandchildren my story, that question had never been asked.

"It was called 'Magical Dreams'."

$$* \quad * \quad * \quad *$$

Turning off the bedroom light, I knew the little girls were going to talk into the night, discussing their own futures, dreaming about their own destinies.

And I knew I could help them with that.

Carol had been surprised about what I wanted to leave my grandchildren in my will.

"But it will be worth a fortune, Mum!"

"It will help them achieve their own dreams," I answered.

Coming Home

I TAKE a break when work is done,
Can't wait to leave the fray;
I'm always told, "You'll have such fun,
It's good to get away!"
I love to just relax and sit,
To visit far-off places,
But oh, I miss, I must admit,
The dear, familiar faces.
When I return, all seems unreal –
Each room looks somehow new.
I rush around and cook a meal –
There's such a lot to do.
Have neighbours fed my cat each day?
They sometimes do forget;
And have the seeds I sowed in May
Begun to flower yet?
So though I love my holiday,
I think it's very plain,
That half the joy of going away
Is coming home again!
                        – Dawn Lawrence.

Grandpa had insisted that I sold that old and rare book. But I never could. It was a part of him that I cherished and I just couldn't bear to be without it.

Instead, I did three jobs to pay my way through university and sold a few stories until I made a name for myself, which eventually helped me to become a successful novelist.

My little cherubs assumed I had sold the book, but I wanted them to have it and find their own magical dreams.

They deserved that.

And me?

I had what I always wanted. My family; my writing to bring joy to others; my beautiful memories . . . and something else that now meant a lot to me.

My very own red bicycle. ∎

iStock.

Aberdovey, Gwynedd

WALKERS, wildlife watchers and water-sports fans will all find something to love about the little harbour resort at the mouth of the River Dovey.

Aberdyfi, as the village is known in Welsh, sits within the Snowdonia National Park, in Cardigan Bay. The harbour is an ideal location for sailing, sailboarding, rowing, canoeing, fishing and boat trips, and tourists come back year after year to enjoy these activities.

Four miles of beautiful, sandy beaches connect it with Tywyn to the north where the Tallylyn railway has its main station.

Further into the countryside, the imposing peak of Cader Idris is a magnet for walkers with a wealth of geological and biological interest where a number of upland plants, such as dwarf willow, reach their southern limit. Walkers might also catch a glimpse of some of the local wildlife, which includes otters, brown hare and water voles. ■

Illustration by Michael Thomas.

Midsummer Magic

by Pamela Kavanagh

NO-ONE could rightly say why the custom of Whalton Bale was known by the older folk of Whalton as Baal Fire. The event itself was little more than a bonfire gathering on the shaggy village green to celebrate the Midsummer Solstice, yet coming from the lips of old Silas Tomms, the very name spoke of ancient rite and mystery, of charms and mystical country lore – all those long-held practices that once were rife in our quiet corner of Northumberland.

The fact that the ritual fell on July 4 – the old-time Midsummer's Eve – added spice to the mix and was guaranteed to send delicious shivers down my sixteen-year-old spine.

"I see they're building the bonfire on the green. It looks to be a big one this time. What a blaze it will make," I said to Mam a few days before the occasion took place.

The throb of excitement in my voice was all too obvious and Mam looked up admonishingly from stoking the oven for the bread.

"Tsk! Listen to you, our Daisy. Dancing round the bonfire! Tes high time you outgrew that sort of thing."

I tightened my lips and carried on kneading the dough. If only Mam knew! Oh, if only she knew how much depended on this year's Baal Fire.

Thump, thump, thump. The everyday task was mesmerising and my mind drifted back to that memorable day last September: golden warmth, the song of larks and all of us bringing the harvest home . . .

* * * *

"Ho, there, Daisy Sharpe. Your bonnet's askew."

I glanced up from where I walked with the others beside the laden wagon, right into the eyes of Jacob Shafto.

So very blue, those eyes. I felt I was drowning in their depths and my heart began to thud as loud as the hoofbeats of the two great Clydesdales that strained into their collars to pull the load. Not that I allowed my feelings to show with Rose Percy sitting up there like Queen of the May on the wagon beside him.

Resisting the urge to straighten my bonnet. I gave back as good as I got.

"That's no surprise, Jacob Shafto, considering the sort of day it's been. We girls have been working, not preening ourselves in front of a looking-glass!"

Jacob laughed.

"Oh, Sharpe by name and sharp by nature! Best bridle that tongue of yours, Daisy. No man wants a scold for a wife."

A throaty giggle escaped Rose's lips. She simpered up at him, delectable little dimples appearing in her cheeks. I could have throttled her for those dimples.

Then I thought how wicked I was. Rose could no more help her plump prettiness and yellow curls than I could help my brown mop, my unremarkable face and frame. I was a farm girl, born and bred, and looked the part, whilst Rose was the milliner's daughter and owned more fancy hats than I'd had hot suppers.

I tossed my head and the unflattering bonnet slipped all the more, falling over my eyes so that I stumbled on the deep-rutted surface of the farm track.

"Careful!" Jacob reached down with a steadying hand.

Oh, how that strong grip burned through the coarse stuff of my sleeve!

I drew a sustaining breath and adjusted the offending headgear just in time to catch the flashing glare of Rose's slanted pussycat gaze, which swiftly became doe-like as Jacob withdrew his hand and turned back to her with a smile.

That was when all the joy faded from the sun-filled day. I was suddenly aware of how my arms and back ached from gathering the prickly stooks of corn and tossing them on to the wagon, of the sweat marks on my bodice and my blistered feet in their unyielding leather boots.

Then someone started singing "Sweet Lemony" and one by one we joined in with the chorus, our voices lifting to the hazy evening sky.

There is nothing like a song for restoring the spirits, and the old familiar phrases soon cast their special magic, spreading balm over my troubled soul.

What did I care if Jacob preferred Rose's sly simpers to my sound good sense? What did it matter that I was only Daisy Sharpe, the girl he'd known all his life, only fit for helping out on the harvest fields?

Jacob Shafto lived at Beamsters, the next farm to ours. It was bigger than Rapps and lay in a lush south-facing valley.

Farmer Shafto's missus by tradition kept bees and sold honey and beeswax at the door. I could not see Rose continuing with the custom, should she become mistress of Beamsters.

As we approached the entrance to the farm, the singing trailed to an end. The wagon drew to a halt in the cobbled yard and folks drifted wearily off to their homes with thoughts of supper and a welcome rest.

Instead of leaving with the others, I reached into my pocket for the bread I had saved, and went to feed the horses that stood patiently for the unloading.

Jacob, lifting Rose down from the wagon as if she weighed no more than a feather, caught my eye and, to my surprise, fetched me a wink.

"They'll love you for that," he called out. "Ain't often they get spoiled."

"Well, it's been a long day for them as well. I reckon they've earned a bit of spoiling," I called back.

Gently the bread was taken from my palm. The horses chewed with relish, their dark eyes appreciative behind their blinkers. I stroked their bony noses and murmured endearments, the way I did to our Bonnie and Violet at Rapps.

"Like the horses, do you?"

I turned to see that Rose was being ferried away in the trap by her papa and Jacob had come to my side.

"Yes, I do."

"What about cows and sheep?"

"I like them as well. You know where you stand with animals – and that's more than can be said for a lot of people!"

The retort was out before I knew it and Jacob, giving me a measured look, lifted his shoulders in a dismissive shrug and went striding off towards the stables, leaving me standing there in the yard wanting to bite off my tongue.

The memory of that wink stayed with me all through the solitary walk home, my thoughts spinning. Had his eyes softened as they watched my unprecedented gesture with the Clydesdales? I doubted it.

Why could I not be more like Rose and smile sweetly at his every word? What made me so much on the defensive, when really I felt the very opposite? It would serve me right if I ended up unwed and unloved like the village schoolma'am, Miss Trimm.

Every girl wanted to be wed, didn't she? To have a cottage of her own with a candle in the window to light her man home of a night? What could I do to make myself softer around the edges so that Jacob would look at me like he looked at Rose?

Evening shadows were now long-drawn across the path. There was a barely discernible whisper of wings and a white owl floated overhead, and in that moment I had my answer.

I'd go to Silas Tomms at his cottage on the heath. It was said he had the Sight. He knew things.

Versed in the old ways, he surely had a charm that could help.

* * * *

Silas Tomms stood in the low doorway of his home and heard me out.

"Rose, is it? Why, then, my maid, tes clear enough. You bide your time till next Baal Fire. You pluck a bloom of the same name from a bush, toss it into the flames and there it be! Romance in ashes."

"But how do I make him turn to me?"

"You wear a chaplet of daisies in your hair."

"Will it work?" I was shamelessly doubtful. "Will it make him love me?"

The cottager looked at me, pity in his rheumy old eyes.

"Maid, the path is set. You cannot change your destiny."

Now he was talking in riddles.

Silas Tomms gave me his gap-toothed smile and watched me walk disconsolately away.

Roses and daisies! What use were these, when I had expected a philtre at the very least? The next Baal Fire was months away.

Rose and Jacob would likely be wed by then, and all my hopes turned to dust.

* * * *

Strangely, no nuptials took place that autumn.

Christmas came, the old year faded, the new one broke and like the dutiful daughter I was, all through the dreary months of January and February winter I milked the cows and tended the dairy and collected what few eggs there were, the hens dwindling off-lay for the winter.

Spring arrived and there were still no church bells for Rose and Jacob.

"Mam," I said. "Do charms work?"

"Well . . ." Mam chewed her lip in thought. "It all depends."

"On what?"

"It hinges on how much a body believes in them. Or perhaps how badly wanted the issue is. Myself, I've steered clear of that sort of meddling and you'd be wise to do the same, our Daisy."

I was silent. I wanted this very much. Early summer was here now and Jacob was still mercifully single. Maybe a thread of magic was holding somewhere. I began to look more kindly on the power of flower lore and set my sights on Baal Fire.

*   *   *   *

A red rose, of course, plucked from the bush that tapped fragrantly at my bedroom window. The daisies were easy. They grew everywhere.

For this Baal Fire I stitched myself a new gown of green calico. Green was a fairy colour and my favourite.

"It becomes you," Mam said, admiring. "What's that in your hair? Daisies? Nice."

In the hidden pocket of my petticoat was the rose, just bursting into bloom.

*   *   *   *

Everyone was gathered on the village green: Miss Trimm, the parson's wife (upright and starchy), the shopkeeper (fat and jovial), gossiping mothers with little ones at their skirts, and the menfolk scrubbed and weather-beaten in tow.

By the pump a clot of village lads stood eyeing the lasses. Rose was there, encased in frothing pink. Of Jacob there was no sign as yet. Probably he was seeing to the milking, for Farmer Shafto was present with his missus, provider of the refreshments set out on a long trestle at the edge of the green.

Over in the shade of the chestnut tree I spotted the grizzle-haired figure of Silas Tomms, watching intently as Farmer Shafto put a taper to the bonfire.

A flighty little wind blew, fanning the flame which caught, crackling, and soon the whole heap of wood was alight and we girls surged forward and danced, laughing, around the roaring mass.

This was old magic, Baal Fire, precedent of the legendary green man and the corn women. As I twirled and leaped in the flickering firelight I surreptitiously tossed the rose into the crimson heart of the blaze.

There, it was done.

I still have to wonder if what followed was pure accident or my wickedness at work.

The wind frisked again, making the flames billow, and Rose's flounced muslin caught a spark.

I let out a shriek of warning and sprang to the rescue, seizing one of the pails of pond water left to hand in the event of trouble and flinging the contents over Rose. The fire was doused at once.

It was all over so quickly I doubt she knew what had happened, but the unexpected deluge of water brought a screech of dismay from her lips.

"You wretch, Daisy Sharpe! What did you do that for? My gown is ruined. And my hair. Oh, and my lovely new bonnet!" She snatched off the latter and flung the sorry mess of soggy straw and ribbons to the ground.

By now the dancing had stopped. There was a pungent whiff of scorched fabric and an array of curious faces. I was probably in a worse state of shock than the drenched, angry figure before me, and began a stammered explanation.

"Rose, I'm sorry. Your frock was on fire. I was putting it out."

"On fire? I think not. You threw that water on purpose, Daisy Sharpe. You farm girls are all the same . . ."

On and on she ranted, and all at once the very sight of her – droplets of water running down her furious red face, pond weed in the hair that in its bedraggled state was every bit as limp as my own, and the gown, a large burn-hole revealing the frilled lace on her pantaloons – was enough to make the ducks on the pond quack in hysterical laughter. I felt my lips twitch.

Rose stamped a foot in outrage.

"Stop that. It's not funny!"

No, it was not funny, and I sobered instantly, the enormity of what could have happened sweeping over me. I opened my mouth to speak but found myself at an uncharacteristic loss for words.

Then, gripped by remorse at what I had done, I lifted my skirts and ran, my only thought to get away from the milling, staring throng of people on the green.

Down the village street I sped, over the stile into our meadow, along the path to the place I had always fled to when I'd been in trouble as a child: a spinney of quivering rowans, the leaves rustling in the evening breeze.

Here I flung myself down in the soft grass and wept.

I don't know how long it was, but through the storm of weeping came the sound of singing and the thud of booted feet on the path. Reaching me, the song died on the singer's lips.

In the next moment a pair of strong hands raised me up to a sitting position. Through a blur of tears I saw Jacob's concerned face.

"Why, Daisy, pet, what ails you?"

The use of the endearment only made me weep all the more.

Jacob sat down beside me on the bank, wrapped his arms around me and shushed me like an infant until my crying stopped. He handed me his kerchief, which was red-spotted and a bit crumpled.

"I hope it doesn't reek of cows. I got delayed with the milking."

"I'm used to cows," I said, gulping down a breath.

"There, then. Mop your tears and tell me what this is all about."

"You won't like it. Likely you'll never speak to me again."

"Try me," Jacob said kindly.

So I told him. I told him about the visit to Silas and its terrible repercussions.

"I didn't mean to set Rose on fire. Oh, how wicked I've been. Ouch!"

I had been crumpling the kerchief into a ball in my hand and felt sudden pain.

"What is it?"

Tenderly Jacob peeled back my clenched fingers and there, across the palm, was an angry blister.

"It must have happened when I was putting out the blaze. Rose's gown was still sizzling and I ran a hand down it to make sure the fire was out. Bits of muslin tore off. She wasn't best pleased."

A twinkle appeared deep in the blue of his eyes.

"I'm sure. Daisy, it was a disaster waiting to happen. Rose shouldn't have worn such a flimsy frock. Come along with me and we'll go back to the farm. There's nothing like a dab of honey for burns."

After Jacob had cleaned and dressed the wound, he looked at me admonishingly.

"Spells and charms! What was the need? Couldn't you see it was you I longed for all along?"

You cannot change your destiny. Silas's words came to me with stunning clarity.

"But it was Rose riding beside you on the corn wagon," I said.

"Aye, it was. She'd complained her boots were hurting her so I gave her a lift."

"She was flirting with you."

"Rose flirts with any lad. Girls like her are not the sort to take as a wife."

"And scolds are? That's what you called me, Jacob. A scold."

"I was but teasing. You were worn out from the day's work on the fields. I should have known better. Daisy, dearest Daisy, can we start again?"

I didn't have to answer because those sweet lips came down on mine as they had so many times in my dreams, and the matter was resolved in a kiss.

$$*\quad*\quad*\quad*$$

Wedding bells rang for Jacob and me later that year.

Of course, we had to wait until after the harvest was in, and this time it was me sitting up beside him on the swaying cart as it lumbered between the shorn fields.

And Rose? She was courting a tailor's lad down Edington way and didn't show up to help with the corn harvest at all.

As we left the church on that perfect day, with lavender skies, the tang of autumn on the breeze, geese winging southwards, I caught Silas Tomms's eye and we exchanged a smile.

Had it all been nothing? Possibly.

Yet there are times at Midsummer, when the moon is bright and round and I stand at the window with my newborn in my arms, I catch on a current of air the whiff of ancient fire and the chanting song of the corn women, and it gives me pause.

Perhaps, just perhaps, there is something in the power of the old magic, after all. ∎

Elizabeth Taylor

Photoshot.

RAVEN-HAIRED beauty Elizabeth Rosemond Taylor was born in London in February 1932. As her parents were both United States citizens, she had dual citizenship and the family moved to America in 1939 as the fear of war with Germany became all too real.

She was a child star – her first foray was "There's One Born Every Minute" when she was just ten years old, but it was her leading role in "National Velvet" at the tender age of twelve, that really put her on the map. The movie was a smash hit and secured her a long-term contract with MGM.

By the age of twenty-two she'd starred in many movies, such as "Ivanhoe". The fact that she could act as well as being considered one of the world's great beauties, ensured her a place in Hollywood.

Other hit movies followed, such as "Giant", "Cat On A Hot Tin Roof" and "Butterfield 8", which won her an Academy Award.

In 1963 she starred in "Cleopatra", where she met her fifth husband, Richard Burton. A few lacklustre movies followed, before Taylor turned in an Oscar-winning performance as Martha in "Who's Afraid Of Virginia Woolf?".

Her personal life often made the headlines – she married eight times, twice to Richard Burton. ■

Illustration by Ruth Blair.

Que Sera, Sera

by Fran Valiant

GWEN beamed in satisfaction. The reception was going splendidly, the guests mingling over the champagne and finger food. Many a lasting relationship, she'd heard, began when people met at weddings. Already she had observed several introductions and watched less-engineered pairings take wing.

It was one of Gwen's maxims that spontaneity took a great deal of planning. Creating the right atmosphere for informality to flourish was an art, but there was always the unpredictable element of chance.

Jonny's golden curls blazed in sunlight. How like his mother he was! Who'd have thought that today had its origins in a classroom years before?

Gwen remembered her first meeting with Hannah as if it were yesterday . . .

*   *   *   *

"We'll start with the girls. When I call your names, sit at the desks, filling in from the front of the room." Miss Probert was young, brisk and efficient.

Many of the staff thus far glimpsed seemed as forbiddingly Victorian as the venerable grammar-school building itself, and Gwen had been thankful to be directed to Form 1A with the lively Miss Probert.

"It will help if you would keep these positions in your classes till half term, so that your teachers can put names to faces. After that, you may sit where you like. We'll know who the troublemakers are by then!" Their form mistress smiled. "When everyone is settled, I want you to turn to your neighbour and shake his or her hand. You'll have five minutes to tell each other a little about yourselves and then I'll ask you to tell me about your partner."

She began reading out the girls' names from her list, and her charges filed into their places at the old-fashioned paired desks, each with its attached twin bench.

Gwen peered shyly at her new classmates.

The girl by the window looked bold and fierce, but Gwen rather admired her neighbour with her freckles and unruly mop of blonde curls.

At her inspection, the curly one gave a broad wink.

"And now the Joneses." Miss Probert sighed. "Always a lot of you in a Welsh school. Anwen, Cerys . . . I see we've got two Gwen Joneses. That might cause some confusion. Gwendolyn, let's have you there, and Gwenllian next to you."

Gwen approached the indicated pair of desks and saw that her deskmate was to be the frowning girl from the window bay. She'd much rather have had the cheery curlytop, but there was no escaping the strictures of alphabetical order.

"Please, Miss Probert?" The frown had been replaced by an ingratiating smile. "I'm Gwendolyn, but I'm usually called by my second name, Margaret," Gwen's namesake gushed. "Would it be helpful if we used that?"

"Thank you, Margaret. So, Hannah Jones next to Gwen, then you, Margaret."

Gwen was delighted to find that she was now paired with the jolly freckled girl, who bounced on to the other half of their shared bench seat.

"Thank goodness!" her new companion whispered. "I was hoping not to end up next to Madam Margaret. She was in my class at primary school and fond of pushing herself forward. Lunch monitor, handing out the milk at break . . ."

"Silence, Hannah," Miss Probert admonished. "You don't want to be the first on my list of students whose names are memorable for the wrong reasons!"

With the roll call complete, Miss Probert asked Hannah to give out sheets of paper so that everyone could create nameplates to keep on their desks.

Brandishing a box of marker pens, she gestured at Gwen, but before she could hand them over Margaret thrust up her hand and volunteered to distribute them.

Gwen found herself the recipient of an eye-rolling grimace and a broad wink from Hannah. She relaxed back into her seat. Form 1A was going to be fun!

*   *   *   *

"Your Susan looks a picture." Hannah's curls were now greying but her cheery expression and boundless energy hadn't faded with the passing years.

"Funny how things turn out, isn't it?"

"We couldn't have planned it any better, could we?" Gwen agreed. "Jonny was brilliant; all his words so clear and sincerely meant. Susan's an unsentimental soul, but I could see she was moved by the joy in his voice."

"He learned elocution from two of the best," Hannah declared, sketching a bow and waving in the direction of her husband.

"You had to master speechifying early on, in your elevated position," Gwen said with a sly nudge.

"After an inauspicious start in Miss Probert's eyes." Hannah chuckled . . .

* * * *

Gwen was dismayed to learn that Hannah had been summoned to the head's study at break. It wasn't the only time since Form 1A that her friend had caught the staff's attention, but it was the first time since they'd been in the Sixth.

Hannah was such a livewire, popular with her peers and always brimming with ideas. What had she been up to?

At lunchtime Gwen found herself dragged into a corner of the common room.

"It'll be announced at assembly tomorrow," Hannah murmured, "but I want you to know. I've been chosen as Head Girl! Peter Everett's Head Boy."

"Congratulations! You deserve it, and so does he." Gwen was thrilled at her friend's success.

"I've got Marker-Pen Margaret as my number two. Mr Evans said it would be good to have a deputy with differing views from my own, so we could represent the whole spectrum of the student body. Pete and I were invited to make recommendations for the rest of the prefects – I've bagged choir leader for you."

"Do you think I'm up to it?" Lack of self-confidence was Gwen's biggest problem.

"You've been doing the job in all but name for ages, and Mr Farrell will be chuffed to have his star A-Level Music student at the helm."

"Sooner you than me for HG," Gwen said fervently. "Having to be the public face of the school and make speeches. Ugh! Good thing you're doing Drama as well as French and RE. Have you heard anything back on your uni application?"

"No, but I'm keeping my fingers crossed for Exeter. Are you still determined to stay in North Wales? Miss Probert was very disappointed when you turned down the chance for Oxbridge."

"I haven't got your adventurous spirit," Gwen admitted.

"We'll be so far apart," Hannah bemoaned. "I wonder if we'll look back years from now and say 'Whatever happened to that girl I used to know in school?'"

* * * *

"Gwen, dear, come and sit down. You've been on your feet long enough." Great-aunt Selena patted the vacant chair beside her.

"I have to see that everybody's taken care of, Auntie. Can I get you anything?"

"The reception won't fall apart if the mother of the bride takes a break." The lady smiled. "Gareth's taken my plate for a refill, but he's chatting up one of the bridesmaids. Susan looks radiant. I'm glad she found the right man at last."

"Have you seen most of the family today, Auntie?"

"Our side, yes, but not many of the groom's people." Selena's eyes twinkled. "I gather he and Susan got together more by accident than design, despite the efforts of certain mothers to manipulate events."

"There may have been a little gentle steering," Gwen protested, "but things have turned out as they should."

"The heart takes its own course, whatever we might do to influence it. You and Hannah have remained such good friends, despite going your different ways. Is she as happy about today as you?"

"When has Hannah ever been less than enthusiastic about anything? Today reminds me so much of her and Andrew's wedding . . ."

*   *   *   *

"I'm so glad you made it!" Hannah enveloped Gwen in a hug.

"I wouldn't have missed it. It's been two years since we last met up."

"It was the end of our first year at college, wasn't it? We took a picnic to Y Felin, and both got sunburn." Hannah chuckled at the memory.

"You'd just met Andrew and I had a summer job so that was the only free day we had in common. I'm glad we've kept in touch by letter. What's this exciting news you hinted at in the wedding invitation?"

"We're going to Africa! Andrew wanted to enter the church but couldn't get a place at theological college. They're desperate for people with practical skills out there and now he's a qualified engineer we're joining a mission.

"He'll be working on a project bringing fresh water to remote villages and doing some lay preaching. It's a former French colony so I can use my languages and do some teaching in bush schools."

"Trust you to end up somewhere exotic, doing something amazing. I'm happy for you," Gwen said warmly, "though it means we'll be even further apart."

"You've got postgraduate studies at Oxford to look forward to," Hannah urged. "Miss Probert would be thrilled to know you got there."

"I wrote to her when my place was confirmed. The last three years have helped my confidence so much."

"We have so much to be thankful for," Hannah said. "Promise me you'll carry on our correspondence. We'll both have new horizons to report."

*   *   *   *

"And so we did." Gwen sighed. "My writing career flourished and I combined it with running an academic library. I met Derek, and the children came along.

Wake-up Calls

MAGICAL the wake-up calls,
Sung by a speckled thrush,
His cheeks puffed up, he sings
with joy,
From a nearby hawthorn bush.
What better way to start the day,
Than a bird who gives his all?
To introduce new mornings with a
Dulcet wake-up call?
Far better than a sudden "bleep"
Or a bell that rings,
Must be when a little bird
Wakes you when he sings!

– Brian H. Gent.

Hannah's two boys were born in Africa, and they came back to the UK when Andrew was accepted for training in the ministry and the children were about to start secondary school."

"You've both made the most of your opportunities," Selena agreed, "but it hasn't always been easy for you to keep up your friendship."

"Fate played its hand at the wrong moment. Just as she left Africa, I was up for that exchange post with an American library and Derek decided to give in to his company's pleas to join them in the Seattle office.

"When we got back from the States, I thought Hannah and I would meet again, but things never seemed to pan out," Gwen added. "It wasn't until the children were grown that our chance came. We still wrote regularly, of course."

Gwen remembered when a letter had arrived one day, not in Hannah's distinctive scrawl, but in Andrew's neat script . . .

*   *   *   *

Trust Andrew to come up with something different! He and Hannah were well matched, Gwen thought, and his idea for a surprise party for his wife's fiftieth birthday was a corker.

She's expecting it to be just family, but I thought that having someone from each decade of her life would be a good way of marking such an occasion. You would be representing the teenage years. It would be great to get you two back together at last! Hannah talks about you often, and looks forward to your letters.

Gwen had cleared her diary for the designated Saturday, and arrived at the appointed time to be greeted by Andrew.

"Hannah's been lured away to the village shop by our youngest, as we're low on crisps," he explained with a wink. "The folks she's not expecting are nearly all here, so come in and meet everyone."

Gwen said hello to a room full of strangers, though she vaguely recognised Hannah's brothers and sisters.

Hannah's elder son Jonny was the image of his mother. She had no difficulty identifying younger son Sam, either, when he preceded Hannah into the lounge on their return from the shop.

The birthday girl emerged to a chorus of "Surprise!"

The delighted shock on Hannah's face said it all. She made a frantic circuit, hugging and kissing familiar faces from yesteryear.

There was a shriek of girlish glee when she spotted Gwen.

"Gwen! You haven't changed a bit."

"Neither have you!" The years vanished in an instant.

During that full and happy day they found time to sit down for a cosy chat.

"Your boys both favour you," Gwen observed.

"Sam has an offer of a job from the company he's doing his industry placement with, for when he's finished uni," Hannah told her, "and he's already engaged to Tricia. He might be young, but he knows exactly where he's going.

"Jonny's different altogether. He's had a series of jobs since college but not settled at any of them. Girls come and go, but there's been no-one special. I suspect that when he finds his niche he'll commit himself one hundred per cent."

"My girls are chalk and cheese," Gwen said. "Debbie adores children and loves her work in nursery care, but I think what she really wants is to find the right man and have a family. Susan's a career woman and when she completes her training she'll be off to London for some high-flying post."

"I wonder what our offspring would make of each other?" Hannah mused. "What makes certain people click and others not?"

"Like Marker-Pen Margaret? We never actively disliked each other," Gwen recalled. "We just didn't gel for some reason. I wonder where she is now?"

"I vaguely remember hearing she'd married some brilliant young boffin. Hey, perhaps my Jonny could be your Debbie's Mr Right? What do you reckon?"

Gwen giggled.

"It would be interesting to get them together and see what happened! One thing's for sure. Jonny and Susan would be a non-starter. She's much too serious and focused to have time for him."

*　　*　　*　　*

"It was that weekend back home in Wales that your grand plan was supposed to come to fruition, wasn't it?" Selena's refilled plate had been delivered by the tardy Gareth and she took an appreciative bite of a cocktail blini.

"Hannah was organising her parents' golden-wedding do, and I wanted the family together for Mam's eightieth birthday," Gwen affirmed. "Trefelin was the perfect venue for both celebrations: not too much travelling for relatives and, with several guests in common, it made sense to book function rooms at the same hotel. That way we could pop into Hannah's party from time to time and vice versa."

"And your unattached offspring would meet at last," Selena deduced. "Very crafty!"

"The best-laid plans." Gwen sighed. "Our angling to bring Jonny and Debbie together was scuppered. She'd just started as nanny with that wealthy Arab family, and they whisked her off to the desert at short notice. Little did we think that things would end up being fixed for Susan instead . . ."

$$* \quad * \quad * \quad *$$

Meeting the parents of one's future son-in-law could potentially be a minefield. What if you didn't get on, casting a blight over decades of family gatherings?

When Susan had informed them that she was engaged, Gwen and Derek were delighted but apprehensive.

Joining Hannah and Andrew for a pre-nuptial lunch would have been a breeze, but instead they were bracing themselves for the hitherto unseen in-laws, Gerald and Meg. Unseen, though not unheard.

Gerald Anson was a well-known radio broadcaster, but Meg was an unknown quantity.

"She does PR, events management and such," was Susan's vague description of her soon-to-be mother-in-law's business.

Hannah and Gwen's machinations to unite their offspring had taken a sideways turn. Jonny's old schoolfriend Toby Anson had been visiting relatives in North Wales on the weekend of Hannah's parents' celebration, and Hannah had invited him to join the party.

Toby was an up-and-coming architect, and he and newly qualified surveyor Susan had found a lot of common ground.

Their meeting resulted in Toby offering Susan a lift back to London, where they were both working, and things had developed from there.

"Here they are at last," Toby said, rising to greet his parents as they entered the smart restaurant where lunch had been arranged.

"Sorry we're late," a voice boomed and Gwen recognised it instantly as that of Gerald Anson.

She was pleased to see the obvious affection which existed between Susan and her fiancé's family. There was much kissing and hugging as they were introduced.

"This is my wife, Meg." Gerald ushered forward a well-groomed woman wearing a stunning designer outfit.

Meg's smile turned to puzzlement as she took Gwen's hand.

"Gwen wouldn't be short for Gwenllian?"

"You've pronounced it beautifully. Susan did mention that you came from a Welsh background."

"What a small world! It's been a long time since Trefelin Grammar School."

"Margaret?" Beneath the expertly applied make-up, Gwen could still see the girl she remembered from that first day in Form 1A.

Wedding plans dominated the conversation across the lunch table, but with the young folk huddled over paint charts for decorating their new home, and Derek and Gerald swapping stories around their shared interest in sailing, Gwen and Meg could chat over coffee.

"When Toby and Susan announced their engagement I offered to organise the wedding," Meg explained. "My company has all the contacts and expertise, but I was told that my services were not required. Our day, our way, as Toby put it. I suppose I am rather pushy sometimes, as you may remember from school."

"You and Hannah were both very forceful personalities in different ways," Gwen said tactfully. "But you made a good team as Head Girl and Deputy."

"She never said so, but I know she would rather have had you. I always envied you, you know," Meg revealed unexpectedly. "We all did. Hannah was the most popular girl in the school and you were her best friend."

"That was an accident of birth or, at least, of our parents' choice of names. We sat together on the first day and it went from there."

"After the first half term we all mixed and matched, but you and Hannah remained together and are still close. Anyway, people admired you for yourself, too," Meg said. "You were quiet, clever and self-effacing, but always willing to help someone struggling with their studies.

"People turned to you if they had a problem, knowing they would find a sympathetic ear and their troubles would go no further," she added. "I always felt I had to push myself forward to be noticed."

"We may not realise how others see us," Gwen mused. "I thought myself very dull and unimportant; too nervous even to venture beyond my own little locality and take up a place at Oxford when it was first offered. Whereas you became Deputy Head Girl, the boss of a thriving business and married to a celebrity."

"Gerald has been very fortunate," Meg replied with a fond glance at her husband. "He was a science teacher, got into schools broadcasting, and it snowballed from there. But you're something of a celebrity yourself. Your literary criticism books are respected and you're an authority on Jane Austen."

"Miss Probert got me started on that when we did 'Emma' for A-Level."

"We didn't need a matchmaker like Emma Woodhouse to get Toby and Susan together!" Meg laughed. "It was fate that they happened to be in the right place at the right time at their first meeting."

Gwen blushed. Perhaps it was just as well that Meg didn't know what Hannah and Gwen had really been planning on that weekend in Wales!

*   *   *   *

Hannah and Meg were heading towards the corner where Gwen and Selena were ensconced.

Since the wedding party had begun assembling at the hotel, the three former classmates had been as thick as thieves. Last night at dinner they had giggled and groaned their way through memories of their schooldays.

Meg had mellowed and Gwen's confidence had blossomed, while Hannah was the same ebullient character she had always been.

Some relationships, Gwen reflected, matured like fine wine, deepening despite years and miles between. Others took longer to get off the ground but were worth waiting for.

She could foresee many more happy reunions now that they had all grown into themselves and found each other again.

Toby and Susan were holding court amidst a crowd of friends, but their eyes were for each other. Across a sea of heads, Gwen could see Jonny in earnest conversation with someone who was hidden from view by the crush.

He had grown into himself, too. The restless young man had found his calling and followed his father into the ministry. Toby had asked his friend to officiate at the service and Jonny had impressed everyone.

"Did you see them at the wedding rehearsal and afterwards at dinner? Jonny looked like he'd been thunderstruck," Hannah commented as the crowd shifted and they could see that Debbie was the object of her son's devoted attention.

"When we were helping Susan get ready this morning," Gwen confided, "it was Jonny this and Jonny that from Debbie."

"She would make an excellent vicar's wife," Hannah declared. "She'd have the mothers' union eating out of her hand."

"Running the toddler group, organising the Sunday school," Gwen agreed.

She and Hannah exchanged triumphant glances. Selena followed their gaze.

"Are you two up to your tricks again?" She chuckled. "Too late! Another marriage made in heaven, if I'm not mistaken."

Just then the best man tapped his glass.

"We're here to celebrate the joining of Toby and Susan. They met by chance but were clearly made for each other. My clerical friend . . ." he nodded in the direction of Jonny ". . . would say that the Lord moves in mysterious ways, and who are we to argue?"

Accident or design; planning or providence? Gwen could only conclude with absolute certainty that what was meant to be would be.

She clinked her glass against those of Hannah and Meg and the three of them toasted the future. ■

The Ultimatum

by Susan Blackburn

XCUSE me, young fellow, would you perhaps assist me, please? My train leaves shortly and I've come over a little dizzy," a voice said.

Bill's heart sank. He only had a few minutes himself to catch his train, and his future happiness depended on it.

He sighed. He hadn't any choice. This could be his grandfather, and he'd like to think if his grandad needed help then somebody would be there for him, too. Manfully swallowing his frustration and with a cheery "Come on, then," he grinned at the old man, gently taking his arm.

They arrived with a few minutes to spare.

Bill settled the old man in his seat and squeezed his shoulder.

"There you go. Sure you'll be all right?"

"Thank you. I'm fine now. My son's picking me up at the other end. He wanted to bring me all the way, but I wouldn't let him. He has enough on as it is.

"My name's Fred Baxter. And you are . . .?"

"Bill Fletcher."

"Well, I can't tell you how much I appreciate your help, Bill. I'm not able to drive any more, you see, so that's why I'm having to use the train. But the station is so much bigger and busier than I remember. I got a bit overwhelmed."

Fred blew his nose on a voluminous white hankie before continuing.

"I thought I was going to miss it, and that would have been a disaster, today of all days. My wife's recovering in hospital after a big operation and it's her birthday today. God bless you, my boy," he added, his voice shaking.

Bill shook Fred's proffered hand, strangely moved.

Fred spoke again.

"I hope you find happiness, Bill. May I give you a word of warning on that score? Don't settle for second best."

As Fred held his hand and stared into his eyes, it seemed to Bill as if Fred could see straight into his mind. He shook his head to clear it.

"I'd better be getting off now, otherwise I'll be travelling with you," he joked, making hurriedly for the door as the shrill sound of the guard's whistle brought him back to the present and his own predicament. "Goodbye, Fred, and good luck."

"You, too, my boy, and thank you so much again."

Illustration by David Young.

With a final wave to Fred as he passed by, Bill was off, desperately dodging through the throng of people.

But despite doing a sprint worthy of the Olympics, he was just in time to see the tail end of his train disappearing into the distance.

He slapped his forehead in despair. That was it, then. He was on his last chance with Polly and he'd just blown it.

He punched in her number and listened to it ringing, his heart thumping.

"Hello, darling. Where are you?" Polly's husky voice, one of the first things that had attracted him to her, came on the line.

"I'm still at the station, Polly. I've missed the train. I am so sorry," he apologised.

"That's it, then." Her icy tones echoed his recent thoughts. "There is no point you bothering to come round now, Bill. I'm not going to turn up late to Suzy's party. I'll go on my own."

There was a decisive click on the line.

Bill stared at his phone. She'd actually hung up on him. He felt suddenly angry. She hadn't even let him explain.

But his anger was short lived. Polly had, after all, given him numerous chances.

This ultimatum had justifiably come when they'd missed the first act of a play Polly had been looking forward to for months. She'd moved heaven and earth to get tickets for them both.

"This is your last chance, Bill," she'd ranted. "Just one more time you let me down and we're finished."

He'd tried to explain that one of his work colleagues had had a deadline and her computer was playing up. He hadn't felt he could abandon her.

"So your work colleague is more important than me?" she'd accused him, tears welling up in those gorgeous brown eyes – eyes he drowned in every time he looked into them.

"No, of course not," Bill replied. "I thought it would only take a moment, but then it took longer and I – well, I –"

"Yes?" Polly said imperiously. "Then you what?"

"Well, I got intrigued with what the problem could be, and I lost track of time," Bill replied sheepishly. "I'm so sorry, Polly."

"And what about when we were supposed to be having lunch with Dad last month?" Polly had said then. "I was dying for you to meet him. And you didn't get there until dessert."

"Oh, Polly, I explained about that. My neighbour was upset because she'd lost her cat. Ellen's a lovely old thing, and I couldn't just leave her. Actually," Bill added, a bit miffed himself now, "I thought you would have understood about that."

"Don't you dare turn this on me. I'm not the bad guy here," Polly had said furiously. "There have been all the other times, too, Bill. You just seem incapable of being on time."

That was when she'd warned him about it being his last chance.

Bill sat on the station bench and sighed heavily. If she'd taken herself off to the party it was hardly worth getting the train to Polly's now. And when she got home, would she even listen to him if he did?

But however mad she was, he couldn't regret helping Fred. He couldn't have lived with himself if he'd walked away.

$$* \quad * \quad * \quad *$$

Whilst all these thoughts were churning through Bill's head, Fred Baxter, after his short journey, alighted from his train and was met by his son, Jack.

They made their way towards the hospital, having stopped to purchase a bouquet of scented roses which he now lay gently in his wife's arms.

They were Vera's favourite flowers. She'd always been thrilled whenever he'd bought her roses, burying her nose in them and breathing in the scent.

"A rose isn't a rose without its perfume," she said now, as she always did.

"I've got to shoot off now," Jack said. "I've got a meeting I can't miss, but I'll be back after that."

"I've come by train today, Vera," Fred said after Jack had gone. "I realised it would be more convenient for Jack picking me up, and it's far more pleasant by train than by bus," he said softly. "I thought I was going to miss it, and I couldn't bear not seeing you on your birthday and bringing you your flowers.

But this lovely young chap, Bill, stopped to help me.

"You know how I can see things, Vera?" He grinned. "Remember how you thought I was really weird the first few times it happened, until you realised how the right word or action could help somebody?"

Fred chuckled.

"Anyway," he went on, "I could see that Bill was a bit mixed up and confused at the moment. I hope that what I said guides him to make the right choice. That it helps him, like he helped me, to find the happiness he deserves."

*　　*　　*　　*

Bill got himself a coffee from the station café, and sat pondering.

It was strange how things seemed to happen whenever he was supposed to meet up with Polly. It wasn't even as if he was a lousy timekeeper.

Whenever he'd been late, it had been for a good reason. He never seemed to have problems getting to work on time, or being prompt for other appointments.

Maybe fate was trying to tell him something.

Then a cold hand clenched his heart at the thought of Polly no longer being in his life.

But hold on a minute, Bill thought, as he took another gulp of his coffee. What would he actually miss about her?

Just lately she seemed to have done nothing but criticise him. She was never happy with what he wore. If he tried to surprise her with an outing he'd arranged, it always seemed as if she would rather be doing something else.

She always chose really high-class restaurants to eat in, which cost a fortune. Not that he minded the expense, but he could never relax. They weren't really him, somehow.

And they could never agree on films any more. She would sigh and fidget all the way through his choices, and she had never forgiven him for falling asleep during some highbrow offering to which she'd dragged him.

He thought back to when they'd first got together, two years ago. She'd started work as a trainee in the law firm he'd worked in since he'd passed his exams. He'd thought all his Christmases had come at once when she'd agreed to go out with him.

She was fun-loving, gorgeous and had a *joie de vivre* about her that was catching. But, over time, she'd changed, Bill realised.

They'd been to dinner a few times with some of their more senior colleagues, and he admitted to himself now that a restlessness and discontentment had crept into her demeanour.

He'd watched her eyeing up the gorgeous décor, the fabulous furnishings, the state-of-the-art kitchens. Then he'd seen her looking around his home, a pouty, discontented look on her lovely face.

At the time he'd dismissed it as him imagining things, because he hadn't wanted it to be true. He hadn't wanted to admit things weren't working any more.

They had been so happy.

"Hello, Bill, mind if I sit here?"

Bill, shaken out of his reverie, looked up to see Ellen, his neighbour, standing there.

"Are you OK?" she asked him.

"Not really," he said.

"Anything I can do to help?"

She sounded so sympathetic, he found himself pouring out his predicament to her.

Ellen listened attentively without interruption.

"So now I'm not sure what to do." Bill stared disconsolately at a piece of litter wafting gently in the draughty station.

"Well, I suppose you have to decide if you still love her or not," Ellen replied gently. "Just don't settle for second best, Bill. You're worth more than that."

Bill felt a tingle up his spine. That was exactly what Fred had told him earlier.

"Thanks for listening, Ellen," he said, giving her a hug. "I suspect I've got some thinking to do."

*   *   *   *

Back at home, Bill poured himself a beer and took it outside.

Looking around, he felt a sense of pride in the cottage garden he'd deliberately designed with conservation more than style in mind.

Watching the butterflies and bees hovering and flitting from plant to plant in the warm evening sunshine, with the scent of sweet williams, honeysuckle and carefully chosen old varieties of rambling roses drifting over to him, he felt a contentment he'd not experienced for a long while.

Polly had been for ever on at him to go for a more designer garden. Just one more way, he realised now, that she'd been trying to change him.

Sadness overcame him as the realisation dawned that he didn't love her any more.

He waited for the pain to hit, but it was relief that actually swept over him.

No more desperately trying to please Polly in the hopes of happiness for them both. He was free now and he would set her free, too, to pursue her future.

Bill grinned as he raised his glass to the gorgeous evening sky.

"Thank you, Fred," he said. "Here's to you." ▮

River Avon At Stratford

IT'S almost impossible to think of the River Avon and its most famous settlement at Stratford-upon-Avon without also thinking of Shakespeare. The Bard of Avon left a wonderful literary legacy that, more than 450 years later, still brings nearly five million tourists a year flocking to his birthplace from all over the world.

Visitors to the town can still see many of the buildings that Shakespeare would have known. You can even visit some of the homes that were occupied by members of his family. His own final home at New Place, Mary Arden's Farm, his mother's childhood home, Hall's Croft, where his daughter once lived and the cottage where his wife, Anne Hathaway, lived as a child are all popular tourist attractions.

On the banks of the river, in the Royal Shakespeare Theatre, the Royal Shakespeare Company still performs Shakespeare's words to packed houses today. ■

The Empire Usherette

by Chris Tomlinson

JANE found out about the event in the newspaper. She hadn't been back to the Empire since she worked there years ago.

The article had made her chuckle.

Come and explore the past of one of the town's most historic old cinemas.

When Jane had first started working at the Empire as an usherette it hadn't been historic at all – it had been state of the art! She remembered the plush velvet seats and the fabulous gilt details on the walls, and the burgundy curtain which used to sweep open across the screen when the B feature was about to start.

The whole place had been magical and modern – that was why she'd applied for a job there in the first place.

Well, that and the fact that she knew that her brother's friend, Andrew, had just started working there as a projectionist. Even now Jane blushed a little just thinking of it.

Now, here she was, standing on the pavement outside the old cinema, although it hadn't been a cinema for many years, having been transformed into a shopping arcade some time in the Sixties.

Jane was part of a little group of people of all ages (all younger than her, she couldn't help noticing). As they gathered, a cheerful-looking man in his forties, wearing a fetching fedora hat and short red scarf, was checking off names on a sheet of paper.

"Ah, good," he said cheerfully after the last straggler had arrived, "we're all here. My name is Rudy, and I will be leading your tour today. Before we make a start I would like to ask if there is anyone here who remembers the building as it once was."

Jane was the only one to raise her hand.

She felt a little self-conscious as the other tour-goers looked at her, although they all seemed friendly.

"Perhaps you can fill us in if there's anything I don't know, or tell me if I get it wrong?"

Illustration by Philip Crabb.

Although there was a jokey tone in Rudy's voice, it was clear that he was genuinely interested in learning from Jane's experience.

"I haven't been back since it became a shopping arcade," she said, "but perhaps some of the inside has stayed the same."

It was nice to feel that her contribution was welcome here, that she might have something to add. However, it wasn't in her nature to seek attention, and it did feel a bit uncomfortable having all the other guests looking at her.

She was soon at ease, however, as the knowledgeable and charming Rudy led them around what had once been her place of work – the most sophisticated picture house in the whole town.

The designers had done a good job of converting the building. What had once been the sloped seating going down towards the screen was now a sort of indoor street, with shops off it on the left and right.

It was better, Jane admitted, that the place was being used than falling down, or being demolished.

At one point they stopped in what was now a jewellery shop.

"I've spent hours poring over the old building plans," the tour guide told the group, "but I haven't been able to get to the bottom of what this room used to be."

"Perhaps it was a popcorn stand?" a European tourist wondered. Jane thought that she might have been Spanish from her black hair and brightly coloured clothes.

"Maybe it was a cloakroom," another offered.

No-one said anything directly to Jane, but she could feel Rudy looking at her, encouraging her to share what she knew.

"No. This was the room where all the usherettes used to sit while the films were on." Jane was surprised at the confidence in her own voice. "I used to come here and chat with the girls once we'd guided the last of the patrons to their seats."

The tour guide smiled.

"Well, I'm glad to have that mystery solved! It just goes to show that you can sit with your nose in a book for a month of Sundays but there's no substitute for personal experience. Perhaps you can tell us a bit more about your days working at the Empire?"

By now Jane was blushing again.

"Well, I don't know about that," she told Rudy, "but I can certainly show you where the projection room used to be. I'm sure I can find my way there again."

*   *   *   *

After the main feature was over and it was time for the filmgoers to leave, most of the usherettes would sit in the staffroom, chatting and having cups of tea. But one or more of them would have to do a quick check of the cinema to make sure that no-one had nodded off during the screening.

"Why do you always volunteer for this job?" her usherette friend Julie once asked her. "No-one likes being woken up when they've been dozing in public, and you're liable to get a confused response from them!"

Jane just shrugged and said she didn't mind.

But the real reason was that, when the film was over, Andrew would take off the film reels, put them back in their cans and pack them away for the next showing.

She also knew he'd be able to see her through the projection window with the lights up, wearing her smart Empire uniform, her hair in perfect order and her manner impeccable as she woke up any snoozing guests . . .

Today, it was easy for Jane to lead the gaggle of tourists from the new jewellery shop to the old projection room. She must have done it at least a hundred times before Andrew finally plucked up the courage to wait for her after her shift with a bunch of flowers . . .

"I thought that perhaps you might like to have an evening out – at the pictures?" he'd said.

It made them laugh in later years that he had chosen that particular activity for their first date.

For their whole married life Jane and Andrew went to the cinema almost every week. They carried on doing it even when they had to start driving to the new out-of-town places when all the old cinemas that they knew and loved from their youth closed down, to be replaced by bingo parlours or restaurants.

And even when the audiences seemed to be getting younger and younger and were sometimes a little bit too rowdy during the quiet bits, they had kept up the custom.

One time, a bunch of schoolboys whistled at a couple French kissing as their train headed off into the sunset and the end credits rolled.

Jane leaned over to Andrew.

"I'm sure this would never have happened in our day!"

Andrew laughed and squeezed her hand.

"Don't you remember the lads throwing popcorn during the Westerns? I'm pretty sure the only reason the cinemas didn't do anything about it is that otherwise they wouldn't have sold half as many boxes from the trays in the intervals!"

She had to admit he had a point there.

They had kept up their cinema-going until the very last months of Andrew's illness, when he was finally too tired to leave their bedroom.

Even then he kept his chin up, and asked their children – hardly children by then – to bring over DVDs for him to watch on the television set that they had moved up into Andrew and Jane's bedroom.

It was just like Andrew to make the best of the situation he was in.

Sometimes Jane worried that she was being unfaithful to his memory by staying in and not going to the pictures any more.

But the thought of going without Andrew by her side was too hard.

✻   ✻   ✻   ✻

Jane was lost in her thoughts as she walked, almost automatically, out of the shop and across the arcade thoroughfare.

What had once been the projection room was now a little book shop with stacks of volumes on the floor and shelves practically heaving with novels. Inside, the comforting smell of old books made the place seem older than it was, and to the untrained eye it would be impossible to know the history of this particular place.

The shopkeeper, a youngish man in a cardigan and half-moon glasses, greeted the group as they entered. He was clearly interested in the history of the building as well.

"I had no idea this used to be the projection room," he confessed, "but I do have a few old things which I found beneath some floorboards when I had a radiator changed. Let me fetch them."

He disappeared into a back room, and when he emerged he was holding a shoebox containing a tobacco tin, a gaudy brooch and some postcards.

"Do you mind if we take these out to have a look?" Rudy asked.

"Be my guest."

One of the postcards was from London. It was addressed to Jim, who had been the second projectionist for most of the time Andrew was working at the Empire. The two of them used to send cards to each other when they went on their holidays and pin the pictures up all over the walls of the room.

On closer inspection Jane discovered that the postcard was signed by Andrew and herself!

"That's my husband and me, sent from our honeymoon!" she blurted out in amazement.

"What a marvellous coincidence!" Rudy said.

The Spanish tourists burst into spontaneous applause, followed by the rest of the group, while the bookseller insisted that she keep the postcard.

After the tour had finished, Rudy came up to her.

"Thank you so much for sharing your experiences with the group," he said. "I'm something of a cinema enthusiast, and I'm particularly interested in films from the Golden Age."

Jane was glad he didn't use the term "olden days".

"A few of us get together once a month and watch a classic film in the community church round the corner. We'd be pleased if you'd join us. Perhaps you could even recount some more of your memories of working as an usherette?"

"I don't know about that," Jane said, nervous once again at being viewed as an expert on something. "Though I have to say I wouldn't mind revisiting some of the films of my youth. It's not the same watching them on your own."

"Splendid." Rudy reached into his satchel and drew out a piece of paper with the date and time of their next screening on it. "I hope to see you there."

$$* \quad * \quad * \quad *$$

By the time Jane got home she felt quite exhausted; it had been a packed afternoon.

Although she wouldn't want to spend every day speaking to small crowds and receiving rounds of applause, the contented feeling she had told her that maybe she should try out some new experiences again, to see what she was capable of.

She chuckled as she thought about the flyer for classic film showings.

Perhaps she should dust off her old usherette outfit to wear while she gave her talk? ■

Gregory Peck

Photoshot.

BORN in April 1916 in California, Eldred Gregory Peck had ambitions to be a doctor. But while at the University of California, Berkeley, encouraged by an acting coach there, Peck became more interested in taking to the stage.

Soon the bright lights of Broadway beckoned and Peck made his debut as the lead in "The Morning Star" in 1942. He was in demand partly due to the fact that he was exempt from war service due to a back injury. But not only that, his rugged good looks and 6 ft 3 in stature made him perfect as a leading man.

Moving to the big screen, Peck's first film was "Days Of Glory", released in 1944. He was nominated for the Academy Award for Best Actor five times – four times in his first five years of film acting!

A versatile actor, he starred alongside Audrey Hepburn in the romantic comedy "Roman Holiday" and a few years later as Captain Ahab in "Moby Dick".

Perhaps one of his best-known roles was as Atticus Finch in "To Kill A Mockingbird", for which he justly won an Oscar.

His career spanned decades across a wide range of genres, including "Cape Fear" and "The Omen", and he later branched out into television work. ■

Practice Makes Perfect

by Maggie Primavesi

ELAINE was sorting out clothes for the holiday when Kate phoned.

"Sorry, Mum, there's a problem. I won't be able to come for the full week. My new manager's arranged an important meeting for Monday afternoon and I have to be there."

"That's a shame," Elaine replied, feeling disheartened and thinking how disappointed Jamie would be. They'd already planned what they would do on the holiday. "I've booked the cottage for the whole week."

"Well," Kate began tentatively, "there is a solution. You could take Jamie down on Saturday on your own and I'll follow later."

As Kate's words sank in Elaine felt her stomach lurch and her legs go shaky. "Well, I suppose . . ."

She just couldn't bring herself to admit to her daughter that the thought of driving anywhere outside their village filled her with foreboding. It had been like that since Len had died.

She'd always felt safe with him sitting beside her and they'd gone everywhere together. He knew instinctively if she felt nervous or uncertain on their journeys, and had the knack of giving her confidence without making it too obvious.

"Good, that's sorted," Kate said, misinterpreting her mother's silence. "I'll tell Jamie. He was so upset when I told him we might have to miss the first few days."

Elaine felt backed into a corner. If she refused to go on her own she'd let Jamie down, yet the thought of driving all that way on the motorway without another adult sent cold shivers down her spine.

"You OK, Mum?"

Elaine managed a tight smile that Kate could picture quite clearly. It was the smile she always gave when someone asked how she was.

"Just a bit nervous about driving that far on my own. It's something I've not done for a long time."

"You'll be fine, Mum. Easy as riding a bike."

I never found riding a bike very easy, Elaine thought. That was something she'd explained to Jamie the other day when he noticed her old bicycle in the

Illustration by iStock.

shed, covered in dust and cobwebs.

She and Len had done a lot of cycling together when they'd first met, but somehow that had tailed off now she was on her own.

"You just need confidence, Gran," he'd replied.

Was that something she'd said to him once? Once confidence was gone, how did you get it back?

She had lost her urge to do things and mix with people since Len died. It was part of the grieving process, she assumed. Things she'd have taken in her stride a short while ago had now become stumbling blocks.

"Shall we give it a good clean?" she'd asked on impulse.

Together they wiped away the dust and polished it.

"It looks great. It's a shame it's stuck in that shed, Gran."

A short while later, ten-year-old Jamie was whizzing up and down her garden path on his bike, wearing his Superman T-shirt.

"Shall we go to the park later?" Elaine suggested after he'd just missed her favourite rose bush for the second time. "You'll have more room to ride there."

"Are you going to bring your bike, too, Gran?"

"I don't think so. Not this time."

"Mr Higgins was on his bike when he asked you to have a cup of tea."

Elaine blushed. She didn't think Jamie had overheard their conversation.

She'd met Bob Higgins at a social club she'd forced herself to join because everyone said it would do her good. He'd asked her to join him several times for a cup of tea in the park café, but so far she'd been non-committal.

"Mum said you should go."

"Oh, did she? You're making me blush," Elaine said, forcing a long-suffering smile. "And your ears have been flapping."

"Grandad used to say that."

"He did," Elaine agreed. "Yes, he did."

That was the trouble. Everyone else's opinions and voices were always ringing in her ears when really the only voice she wanted to hear was Len's.

It was strange how something that used to be so familiar to her had become so hard to recall. The words and phrases he used were still in her head, but not the sound of his voice.

"Are you feeling sad about Grandad?" Jamie got off his bike and stood next to her.

"Yes, I am," she replied. "I miss him."

"Me, too." Jamie cuddled into his gran.

Strangely, her grandson was the only person she could admit that to. She didn't need to tell him she was fine like she did with other people.

"Keep your pecker up, Gran."

She smiled to herself. Pecker was another of Len's funny words, and she had no idea where it came from. It didn't sound patronising when Jamie said it. It just sounded, well, like Len.

*   *   *   *

Watching Jamie racing about the garden on his bike, it was hard to believe he could hardly wobble along on his own once. It had taken hours of his grandad patiently walking alongside him, gripping the seat to steady it and whispering encouragement.

"Have a magic mint. It will help you to concentrate. Try to relax your hands on the handlebars a bit. Now pedal as hard as you can. Quick, before those Martians get you!

"Well done!" he'd cried when Jamie made it to the end of the path on his own. "It's only a matter of confidence. You've done it!"

"Did I get away from the Martians?" Jamie asked.

"I think you did. You were well ahead of them."

Elaine had made a cake to celebrate and they'd all sat out in the garden and toasted his success with lemonade.

"What's your super power today?" Elaine asked him as the rose bush narrowly escaped another battering.

Jamie tapped the side of his nose mysteriously like Len used to.

"I'm going to give you some confidence, Gran."

*   *   *   *

Practice makes perfect. Wasn't that another one of Len's sayings? Elaine was sure it was.

Her hands were shaking a bit as she took her bike out of the shed and wheeled it across the road into the park. It was still early and she hadn't eaten breakfast yet.

There was a little path behind the trees, out of sight of most of the dog walkers, where she could practise.

At first she couldn't bring herself to get on the bike. She felt sure she'd fall off as soon as she was up there. Then Jamie's words came back to her.

"You just need confidence, Gran."

Eventually she hoisted herself up on to the seat and gripped the handlebars as if her hands were glued to them.

"Right . . . pedal," she told herself. "The Martians are coming."

It felt wobbly at first and she had to put her foot down once or twice to steady herself.

How am I going to change direction, she wondered. There's no way I can take my hand off to indicate.

That was when she heard the voice behind her. She couldn't be sure, but she had an idea whose it would be.

"One step at a time. Don't worry about that yet. Just keep going straight ahead."

Elaine pedalled as hard as she could. It was beginning to feel good.

I'm starting to get the hang of it, she thought.

The wind was in her hair and she felt more carefree than she had for a long time. She was enjoying herself so much she almost didn't notice the cyclist coming from the opposite direction.

Elaine braked hard, the bike swayed from side to side, but she managed to remain upright.

"You were going like a bat out of hell along there!" Bob Higgins laughed good-naturedly.

"The Martians were after me!" Elaine laughed.

"In that case, I think you need a bacon roll and a mug of tea in the café."

Elaine realised how hungry she was.

"I think I do," she agreed.

Over breakfast she explained why she was cycling in the park at that time in the morning on her own.

"It must sound odd," she said, "a person my age learning to ride their bike again, but I don't like to disappoint my grandson."

"Not at all," Bob replied. "When I was widowed I found it hard to walk round the supermarket on my own. I think you're doing really well. As for the driving, I could take you out for a practice run on the dual carriageway. See if we can find any Martians there."

"Brilliant!" Elaine exclaimed. "How about this afternoon?"

"The sooner the better," Bob replied. "Before you have time to start worrying about it."

"Do you know," Elaine began, "those are the same words Len used after I passed my test and first drove the car on my own."

Elaine walked home pushing her bike, but she had a spring in her step and her face was flushed from the exercise. She didn't feel up to riding along the busy, main road yet, but that would come in time and she was looking forward to the drive that afternoon.

*   *   *   *

The holiday came round really quickly.

"We're going on the brown snake in a moment, Gran." Jamie had the road atlas open on his knee. He'd invented the game after Elaine told him about her practice runs with Bob.

"That's right, one of the little roads. I need to concentrate."

They'd taken the scenic route, keeping away from the motorway. Elaine thought that would be easier till she got used to driving again. Now they were stuck behind a tractor.

"It helps to suck a mint. Road clear behind, Gran."

Elaine checked just to make sure.

"You're doing great, but this is a bit slow." Jamie put on his robot voice. "Prepare to overtake. Foot down. Relax hands on the steering wheel."

Elaine sailed past the tractor. Butterflies were still performing acrobatics in her stomach, but she was getting there.

*   *   *   *

"Well done, Gran! Do you need petrol?"

"Do you mean me or the car?"

"You, of course." Jamie giggled. "I think you're looking a bit peaky."

Elaine smiled to herself. Peaky was one of the words Len used to say. It was amazing how Jamie just picked things up and stored them inside his head, like a little sponge soaking up words.

"Just a bit tired. Nothing that a scone and a nice pot of tea won't put right."

"Good! Approaching tearoom. Turn left at teapot sign."

Elaine smiled again. He'd also inherited his grandfather's sense of humour. The way he'd made jokes to put her at ease.

Her heart gave a little twist.

"You know, Gran, I'm really looking forward to this holiday. We'll have such fun going on drives and bike rides."

"Yes, I really think we will, Jamie."

Elaine was thinking also of the bike ride she'd arranged with Bob when she got back.

She'd have fun on that, and the ones to follow. ▥

Illustration by Martin Baines.

In The Mustard Fields

by Tessa-Jo Stone

CAROLINE was cleaning the slates. Most of the children had forgotten that they were supposed to bring a rag from home and relied upon spit and sleeve.

She usually saved William Manning's slate till last. Here it was, covered in mathematical calculations – long division tonight. William was so far ahead of the class that he invented his own problems while the others finished their tasks.

It was a pleasure to check them after the children clattered out at the end of the day: she rarely came across any errors. However, young William's arithmetic was destined to remain on the slate that night.

She had opened the door to let in some air. Even now, the day was hot and the windows were too high to allow for any breeze. As she bent over the slate, a shadow fell across her desk. Startled, Caroline looked up to see a young man.

He was thin, with dark eyes and a short black beard. A school inspector? No, he wore no suit, and she could see a patch on his sleeve, very neatly done.

"Jed Manning," the man said. "Can't shake hands, I've been in the field."

Caroline inclined her head.

"I am Miss Purley. How may I help you? Are you related to William?"

"Brother," was the curt reply. "I am come to tell you that William is leaving school at the end of the month, on his tenth birthday."

Caroline was dismayed. William was her keenest pupil. She couldn't lose him!

"What of his parents?" she inquired.

"Died in the 'pox plague of Seventy-one. My older brother also. That is why I need young Will at the farm."

This was what Caroline's father had predicted. He was convinced she would not succeed: country children were more useful in the fields than the classroom.

Her dream had always been to teach, but not as a governess. She wanted children from poor families to have the privilege of an education and had been appointed as schoolmistress in Darrow's Mustard Farm School.

But to have a child leave so soon after her arrival! Could she not prevent it?

"Mr Manning, please reconsider," she pleaded. "William is entitled to be in school until the age of thirteen. Haven't you heard of the Education Act? I believe he could enter one of the professions, with your support."

A thought occurred to her.

"Have you difficulty in finding the weekly penny? If so . . ."

"No," Jed replied with a sad shake of the head. "That is not the case."

And before Caroline could say any more, he turned and left.

Caroline spent a restless evening pondering the problem. There must be something she could do! If she couldn't help children like William, what was the point?

Before she left home, her father had given her a sum of money.

"Keep it for your journey home," he said. "It may be sooner than you think."

Determined to prove him wrong, she had spent it all on a Norwich shawl that she'd seen in a fashionable shop. It had been a promise to herself that she was an independent woman who was going to succeed in her chosen path.

Glancing at the shawl, its intricate design in rose and moss green, Caroline came to a decision. She would visit the mustard farm and speak again with Jed.

William was too delicate to be labouring in the fields all day long. There had to be a compromise.

*　　*　　*　　*

The farm lay within walking distance, although the road was dry and dusty and Caroline's skirts were in a disgraceful condition by the time she reached the farmhouse door. The sun beat down upon her, and she felt flustered and uncomfortable.

The mustard crop was ripening ready for harvest in late September, but she couldn't see any workers. The plants were taller than she was, and limited her view. Each was slender and graceful, but the whole field seemed a strange, rustling forest – all to be cut down by hand with scythes.

How would poor William fare? He was a scholarly boy, totally unsuited for such an occupation. The heat was making her feel faint, and she was a grown woman!

Caroline heard Jed Manning's voice before he was visible, evidently talking to another man.

Scraps of the conversation drifted towards her.

". . . will take some of this land off your hands," the second voice said. "The crop is likely to be poor this year. Your plants are wilting in the heat and look ready to die."

She moved near enough to see the two men. The elder one was leaning over a fence, waving his hand in the direction of a field where mustard plants lay battered and flat, their pods shrivelling on the earth.

"More of this wind and drought and there will be little worth harvesting," he went on. "I can help you out, Manning, shorthanded as you are. I'll offer a good price."

"A kind offer, Ezekiel, but I have no intention of selling."

"Lad, you were not brought up for the farm. It should have gone to your brother, God rest his soul. Can't you see I'm trying to help?"

"I thank you, but I have made up my mind, and you will not persuade me to change it. Good day to you."

Jed whirled round, and caught sight of Caroline. The man across the fence caught her eye and shook his head slightly as he ambled away.

The conversation was fruitless. Jed looked hot and tired, in no mood to hear her. She pleaded William's cause in vain. Did he not care about the boy?

Next morning, her head ached. Never had the pounding of the steam stampers seemed louder.

Thump, thump, thump, crushing the mustard seeds to powder, with it crushing her hopes and ambitions. She was glad when the day ended and her scholars tumbled out of the schoolroom.

William, pale and anxious, hovered by her desk.

"Miss, I won't be here next week. I'm sorry, but I'm needed at the farm."

He flexed a tiny muscle in his skinny arm.

"Don't worry about me, miss. And take no notice of our Jed. He sounds raw, but he's just worried. Farm isn't making much money. We never know from one year to the next what Darrow's are going to buy from us."

He scuttled away, and Caroline was left listening to the relentless hammering of the machines. She took her pen from the inkstand and wondered about drafting her letter of resignation.

She could not regret buying the Norwich shawl, but now she did not have enough money to travel home. Would she have to sell it, or apply to her father for assistance?

A sharp rap at the door interrupted her thoughts.

She was surprised, and even a little disappointed as another young man bounced in, holding out his hand.

"Frederick White at your service, ma'am."

Mr White had sharp grey eyes and a thatch of fair hair, well slicked back. Caroline admired his brown tweed suit and the mustard yellow cravat round his neck.

It appeared that he admired her, too.

"It is a pleasure to meet you, Miss Purley!" he cried. "I declare you are a great improvement upon the previous incumbent."

Caroline smiled at his enthusiasm.

"I am indeed Miss Purley. But how did you know my name? We have not been introduced."

"I make it my business to know everything that happens at Darrow's," he replied smartly. "I'm one of the new advertising agents. The future of the world lies in advertising, Miss Purley."

"I am bound to disagree," Caroline said. "I believe the future of the world depends upon education."

Frederick's grey eyes twinkled as he hefted a large canvas bag on to the teacher's desk. He drew out a large sheaf of picture papers.

"Education, ma'am!"

Caroline gasped in delight as she beheld fact sheets – information on all the countries in the world which were supplied mustard by Darrow's; illustrated pages on hobbies and useful pastimes for boys and girls; story sheets; fairy tales and adventures. She spread out the papers reverently.

"Mr White, how did you come by these?"

Airily he explained that the papers were intended to be packed with grocery orders and delivered to households. He tapped the side of his nose.

"I knew the school could use them, so I kept a few back."

"I am most grateful," Caroline breathed, dazed with excitement.

The young man seemed to see his advantage.

"I wonder, Miss Purley, whether you would care to come for a drive in my new pony and trap? I could show you a little of our beautiful countryside."

She hesitated, but not for long. She was a schoolmistress, a respectable employee of Darrow's, and so was Mr White. They could not be accused of impropriety.

"Thank you," she said. "I shall be pleased to accept."

Hay Making

THE holidays I loved the best
When I was a young child,
Were spent with cousins on their farm
Where we simply ran wild!
The thrill of seeing the hay being cut
With clouds of dust that rose
To billow in the clear blue sky
And stick to skin and clothes!
And when the stacks had all been built,
The men's hard labour done,
We'd have a sumptuous picnic feast
Spread out under the sun!
And oh, that smell! That heady smell
Of sun and new-mown hay,
And if I close my eyes right now
I'm right back there today!

– Eileen Hay.

Only when he had gone did she find herself wishing that it had been another young man who had made her such an offer.

*   *   *   *

She found Frederick an agreeable companion with a fund of amusing stories, mostly centred upon himself and his value to the company.

Indeed, if Frederick White were to be believed, he was old Mr Darrow's right-hand man, most valued employee and confidant.

At the end of the week, William left school with great regret. Jed came to meet him, touched his cap and exchanged a few polite words with Caroline.

She did not try to change his mind. She realised that times were hard, and the talk at Darrow's was that the yields would be poor this year. The heat showed no sign of abating: there had been no rain for weeks.

The following evening she was sitting in the schoolroom with the door open, waiting for Frederick to call. The pony and trap now boasted a yellow canvas

iStock.

cover with the name *Darrow's* emblazoned upon it.

Frederick himself sprang into the room with an air of excitement. Caroline was a little weary of his endless exuberance.

"Caroline, we shall inspect the mustard farms tonight," he announced. "I have some most important information, not to be repeated."

"Please be prudent, Frederick," she felt impelled to reply as he helped her into the seat, which was dusty and dirty. Caroline was glad she had decided against wearing her lovely shawl.

"I'm sure you can be trusted," Frederick said, oblivious to her discomfort as the pony trotted briskly along the dry rutted track towards Manning Farm.

Ahead of them were two figures; one tall, one short. The elder had his arm around the child and they were laughing together. Jed and William!

William was carrying a roughly made fishing rod in one hand and a jar of tiddlers in the other.

She begged Frederick to turn back but he ignored her.

"Cheer up, Caroline. I have not yet told you my news! That will be enough to put heart into Mr Manning, even if it's too late to do William any good."

$$* \quad * \quad * \quad *$$

Later that evening, Caroline mulled over what Frederick had confided in her. If only she could tell Jed!

Restless, she decided to walk along the lane that led to the schoolhouse. The evening was cooler than of late and purple clouds were massing in the sky.

Caroline turned back to fetch her Norwich shawl. It gave her courage to feel its heavy folds across her shoulders.

She unlocked the classroom door, and saw, piled up at the end of each long row of desks, the illustrated papers Mr White had brought. She was grateful to him for that, at least.

An idea struck her, and hastily she gathered up a selection of papers and set off down the lane to Manning Farm. William, she was sure, would enjoy them and she could see how he was faring.

Her tentative knock at the door brought William. To Caroline's relief, he looked delighted to see her. She gave him the papers and he fell upon them like a beggar with bread.

Alas, a heavy tread along the hall made Caroline's hand shake. Jed was scowling as he folded his arms across his chest.

William showed him the papers but Jed plucked them out of his hands.

"Thank you, miss, but we have no need of them."

William looked pleadingly at his brother, and Jed had the grace to relent.

"Very well. You may keep these."

Turning to Caroline, he spoke coldly.

"Thank you, Miss Purley, but we will have no more favours from you."

"I'm so sorry," she began, but the door was shut.

She trailed miserably away along the farm track.

Halfway back to the school, she heard a rustling amongst the mustard plants and spied a shadowy, stealthy figure scuttling away. Then a distinctive odour stung her nose. A tiny plume of purple-grey smoke was curling lazily into the air.

Fire!

She darted into the crop and saw small blades of flame creeping along the edge of the field. Caroline knew at once that she must put them out before they took hold. Thankful she was wearing stout boots, she stamped on the little flames, sobbing and shouting for help as she trampled blindly along the path of the blaze.

It was going too fast for her. The blades were becoming larger spears, the smoke was darkening, and still nobody came. No time to run to the farm, no time to send for the fire cart.

At the edge of the field the crop was meagre – but how could she stop the blaze from reaching the larger plants? What else could she do? The crop would be ruined, Jed's livelihood gone, William's future in jeopardy.

In an instant, the answer came. Her shawl! Her beautiful, beautiful shawl.

Caroline hurled it from her shoulders and beat it down, again and again. Black smoke choked her as she fought the conflagration. Could she win? Not alone. But she would never stop.

Dimly she became aware of noises, of men shouting, heavy feet running. Then Jed was there, holding her, and she heard William. Was he crying?

A clap of thunder startled the company, followed by the sweet sound of pattering rain. The last thing Caroline remembered was the sight of a harmless wreath of smoke rising into the air from a few charred fragments. All that remained of her Norwich shawl.

*　　*　　*　　*

"There, now," a deep, comforting voice said. "All shall be well. You have saved us, Miss Purley."

Caroline woke up in her lodgings to find Jed sitting beside her, and in a corner, a nurse, sewing quietly.

"Ten minutes, Mr Manning," the nurse said. "Miss Purley needs to rest. I shall fetch you both some tea, and then you must leave."

Jed drew his chair nearer to Caroline's and patted her hand.

"We have not started well, Miss Purley."

"Caroline."

"Very well. Caroline. May I make amends now by explaining? Please hear me."

Caroline nodded.

"I took William from school to help with my accounts. I cannot for the life of me cast a row of figures and make them balance. He is my clerk."

Jed shrugged.

"I regret it. Guilt made me hasty and ill tempered. Believe me, Caroline, I do not wish the boy to work in the fields. He helps a little, at his own volition."

She murmured assent.

"It was Will who heard you calling. He likes to open his window and view the crops. He takes pride in the farm, though that is no excuse for removing him from school."

He glanced down but continued.

"Farming is a precarious business and I have Ezekiel pressing me to sell him my land. If I only knew what Darrow's were going to buy, then I could make better provision."

Caroline began to wonder if Frederick White had told others about his discovery. Maybe she was not the only one aware of Mr Darrow's plans. Frederick was well-meaning but she doubted his discretion.

"I think I may have an answer for you," she began, conscious of her sore throat and husky voice.

Jed gripped her hand.

"Don't try to talk, Caroline."

"I must. But do me the grace of looking surprised when Mr Darrow calls the company together."

Jed's smile lit up his face and warmed her heart.

"I have lately found out . . ." She was blushing, but continued. "Next year, Mr Darrow is to issue a contract to each farm."

Jed started in surprise.

"He is a fair man and knows the uncertainty of his farmers' position. He will guarantee a minimum purchase at a fair price."

"So, if Ezekiel were to have my land," Jed exclaimed, "he would increase his share of the profit. He must have known this! It was surely one of his men who set fire to my field."

The nurse returned with the tea and tactfully withdrew. Caroline was grateful for the hot liquid on her dry throat.

Jed released her hand and stood up.

"I think we understand one another now. I thank you most truly, Caroline. Maybe, when my accounts are in better shape, William could return to school."

"I should be glad to see him."

"Me, too?" The dark eyebrows rose, questioning.

"You, too, Mr Manning."

"And with my first profit," he continued, "Will and I would like to escort you to town where we will purchase the finest shawl that ever was made."

"I shall look forward to that," was the heartfelt answer. ■

Audrey Hepburn

Photoshot.

ONE of the world's most successful actresses, Audrey Hepburn was born Audrey Kathleen Ruston in May 1929, in Brussels. She is regarded as a fashion icon to this day.

With her natural grace and elegance, it's not surprising to learn that she studied ballet in Amsterdam and later in London, appearing on stage before making her feature film debut in "One Wild Oat", in an uncredited role.

She first appeared on Broadway at the age of twenty-two, where she starred in "Gigi". It wasn't long before she was snapped up to star in "Roman Holiday", alongside leading man Gregory Peck.

Proving her great dancing abilities, Hepburn teamed up with Fred Astaire in the musical "Funny Face". She hadn't only light-hearted roles, however, as she also starred in Leo Tolstoy's "War And Peace".

Hepburn is remembered fondly for her role as Holly Golightly in "Breakfast At Tiffany's", starring alongside George Peppard, and captivated audiences with her part as Eliza Doolittle in "My Fair Lady".

She is one of the few actresses to win an Emmy, Tony, Grammy and Academy Award.

She became a goodwill ambassador for UNICEF in the late 1980s, and acting took a back seat. The legacy of her work to help children continues to this day and she will, of course, always be remembered for that "little black dress". ∎

Going Places

by Jessma Carter

MELISSA watched at the window for Robbie and went to switch on the kettle when his van reversed into the driveway. It had been a long day; clouds of memories had come and gone. One moment she had wanted to run from them, the next moment she had wanted to embrace them.

It had been a shapeless day since Robbie left that morning. The radio, usually a background murmur, was loud and intrusive with bad news. There was no singing that morning in the kitchen, no complaints, no teasings, no requests.

There was a loud swish as she swilled out the teapot. Every other sound – her footsteps, the hum of the stove, the clatter of cups – was intensified, for she was alone. The leaving had come too quickly.

* * * *

"It feels like twins." The doctor spoke gently as he watched Melissa's reaction. A surprise like that can take some time to absorb.'

"I'll arrange a visit from the district nurse. She'll keep an eye on you and will be there to help you after the twins are born," the doctor added.

Melissa's mind was in a whirl. Names, cots, clothes, buggies: all would have to be reorganised. She couldn't wait to get home to share the news with Robbie.

They both read books about twins.

Never call them "the twins", they read. *You must give them their names to make them feel special individuals.*

"That's OK." Robbie was always good-natured. "It will be Geoff and Alex on the days that we like them, or Geoffrey and Alexander when they're naughty."

He looked at Melissa's worried face and gave her a hug.

"You'll be a great mum, Melissa. Nature must have known that. You planned one and got one free!"

Now, 18 years later, Geoff and Alex were gone, their cases behind them.

Having children grow up in tandem, as Melissa and Robbie had discovered, had its ups and downs. Leaving home together was a definite down point for Melissa on that empty morning after their departure.

* * * *

They had driven the boys to Edinburgh on Melissa's birthday, had lunch and then all gone to see the film "Gregory's Girl" before dropping off the boys at the

Illustration by Philip Crabb.

flat they would be sharing.

Edinburgh was a city familiar to them and only an hour away by car, but Melissa could think only of the many murder mysteries she had read that were set there; how students weren't as wise as they thought and how eating disorders could happen to the best of people, even those brought up on a wholesome diet.

Had she reminded them that money didn't grow on trees and that there was such a thing as a laundry? Not to mention the sadness she felt after watching the film. Would their boys meet the right girl? It was the Eighties and so much had changed since her young days.

Robbie was his usual self as he came home after work.

"Been all right?" He gave her a grin. "Are you packed up and ready to go?"

Melissa nodded.

It had been Robbie's idea that they go off for the weekend to Oban, to where they had spent their honeymoon. He'd booked in at the hotel that they had stayed in. It faced the sea and the promenade where people strolled until sunset.

Robbie went to change his clothes and came back.

"Not even a wet towel lying in the bathroom. This is luxury, Melissa."

He shook his hair into place, grinning and looking the spitting image of Geoff.

∗　　∗　　∗　　∗

It wasn't quite sunset when they arrived in Oban.

The islands in the Firth lay like a promise on the water as Melissa and Robbie recalled the boat trips they had taken while on honeymoon. They watched together as stars appeared one by one, and they talked quietly of their shared past.

"I remember you in primary one," Robbie teased. "I remember you bringing messages from your teacher to my teacher. You always looked so small and solemn."

"I remember taking messages. It was regarded as a privilege and only those whom Miss Pringle called the reliable girls were allowed to do it. Do you remember Lorna? She was always my buddy when we were given classroom duties. She came with me. Or, rather, I went with her. She was the one in charge."

Lorna Jackson! Melissa smiled at the memory.

On their first day at school, Lorna had been sent to sit beside her. By way of introduction, Lorna had laid her bulging new pencil case on the shared table.

"That's my new pencil case. Borrow a pencil if you need one. There's lots in there."

Melissa had returned the friendly gesture by opening her mouth and pointing to a gap in the front.

"That came out last night."

Lorna peered into Melissa's mouth.

"That must have been sore." She screwed up her face in sympathy.

It had made for an easy start to a long friendship.

"Do you still keep in touch with her?" Robbie asked. "I know you used to send her a card at Christmas. I was asked yesterday to look at her mother's old house and suggest a bit of modernising work on it."

"That's interesting. The last time I heard from her, her mother had gone into a home and the house was left empty. You must have seen the cards I've had from her at Christmas?"

"Yes, but I never took much interest, to tell you the truth. I always thought she had a good notion of herself. Never really took to her."

"She's travelled the world," Melissa told him. "Done really well for herself. She was working for a big company in Hong Kong, the last I heard."

"Well, it seems she's coming back to stay in her mother's house. You'll be able to catch up with her news quite soon."

"Coming home? To live?" Melissa looked at first pleased, then doubt crossed her face.

"What's the matter?" Robbie knew her moods so well.

Melissa stroked Robbie's hand.

"I think I was jealous of her, even although she was nothing but nice to me. She'll maybe turn out to be one of those very successful women and I'll feel she's a stranger."

Robbie put his arm round Melissa's shoulders.

"But she hasn't brought up two fine young men."

They walked along the promenade, thinking of the boys, watching the sun redden and sink below the sea.

"Lorna was the one who said I should call myself Mel instead of Melissa. She said Melissa was a Greek word for a bee and I thought she was so clever to know that, though I didn't much like the idea of being called after a bee."

"What's wrong with that? It reminds me of honey." Robbie gave Melissa's hand a squeeze. "It would have given me an excuse to call you 'honey' if I had known that all those years ago."

*   *   *   *

A few days after Robbie and Melissa came back from their break in Oban, Robbie was able to tell Melissa that Lorna Jackson had visited her parents' old house and discussed alterations with him.

Melissa was surprised and immediately wanted more information.

"Well?" she began. "What was she like? Was she the way you remembered?"

"More or less. A bit older. That's all."

"Honest to goodness, Robbie! You didn't notice if she looked smart, if she had put on weight, or if she had aged well? You didn't ask if that's her finished working and if she means to stay on here?"

Robbie carried on sipping his tea.

"I tell you what, Melissa. Just you give me a questionnaire and I'll hand it over to her." He paused and smiled. "She said she was going to call, so you can ask her yourself."

The bell rang.

"That'll be her. She said she'd call after teatime."

Melissa rolled her eyes.

"You might have warned me," she muttered as she went to the door, patting her hair and pulling down her sweater to sit more neatly over her trousers.

"I just did!" Robbie laughed.

*   *   *   *

It was an easy meeting. They were still talking when Robbie appeared two hours later with a teapot in one hand and a tray with cups in the other.

Much later, he was aware of Melissa's restlessness as she lay beside him in bed.

"I thought you would be sleepy after all that blethering," he teased.

Melissa wanted to talk.

"She's getting married. She's met this widower from Perth. He was out in Hong Kong – something to do with insurance. They're going to live here. He's got a son and a daughter and Lorna will have her hands full looking after them. Can you believe that, Robbie?"

"I can. If you say so."

"She thought Alex and Geoff looked bright and eager. That's what she said when I showed her the photo we took when they left. She thought I had done things the right way round. Had my family first. She sounded kind of regretful that she hadn't had children."

Melissa paused.

"She asked if I remembered how surprised she had been when I said I was going to marry you," she added. "She wanted to apologise for that."

"For what?" Robbie was drifting into sleep.

"For thinking I was doing the wrong thing. She thought I should have gone on to do some training. Perhaps gone to university, like her."

"Maybe she was jealous of that job you had at the gardening centre. All those lovely plants to look at and all those sturdy young men that grew them. I know I was jealous."

"Really? You never told me that before."

"Well, I was." Robbie turned towards her. "I still get jealous sometimes."

He put his arm round her.

"Let's get to sleep."

But the past was intruding and making it difficult for either of them to sleep. Eighteen years seemed like yesterday. Robbie seemed not to have changed at all, Melissa thought, and here he was saying that he could still be jealous.

She sat up in bed.

"Are you saying you don't trust me?"

"Of course not. I'm saying I didn't trust those gardeners you used to work with at the garden centre. They looked a risky lot to me."

Melissa laughed.

"Risky? They were ordinary young men, keen to do their job and learn about plants." She settled down under the covers. "You know what I like about you? You make me laugh."

She could feel Robbie smile.

"That's not much. Anything else?"

"Everything else."

"Me, too. In fact, now that I've got used to you, I like you even more."

$$* \quad * \quad * \quad *$$

"You've not had a job since the boys were born?" Lorna asked.

"Not outside the home. I've kept accounts, answered the phone, chased up supplies for Robbie's work, but never really followed up on learning about plants, which is what I would have done had I not fallen for Robbie."

"I think you're talking nonsense, Melissa." Lorna sounded just as bossy as she had been at school. "Look at your garden. I'll bet it wasn't Robbie that designed that, or chose the plants. I remember when you first came to this house there was no garden at all. Just a wilderness of grass. I'd call that work, Melissa."

Melissa looked out of the window and could still see the wilderness of grass, could remember clearly laying the boys on a rug while she dug and planted, bit by bit.

She remembered how the garden changed around them and their needs. A fence to keep them safe, then a large garden hut. Letting the twins plant quick-grow crops like beans so that they would take care to keep off the vegetable plot. Planting apple and pear trees for them to pick fruit from and climb.

Lorna's voice broke into her reverie.

"It's your turn for a change, Melissa."

"It's your turn, too, Lorna. You'll soon find out that looking after two children could be called work."

$$* \quad * \quad * \quad *$$

It was only a few weeks later when Melissa rang Alex. He was usually more awake than Geoff first thing in the morning.

"I'm coming to Edinburgh today. I thought I'd take you both out for a good lunch."

"Great, Mum." It sounded like a yawn at the other end of the line.

"I'll call at the flat around noon. Would that be all right?"

"The flat?" Alex was suddenly wide awake. Melissa knew a visit from her would panic the boys. "No need for that, Mum. We'll just meet you."

"No, no. I'll call. I've some stuff to drop off. I've some sweaters you left behind."

Melissa put down the phone. She imagined the scene in Edinburgh: Geoff hauled out of bed, a slight frenzy as the boys cleared up, clothes kicked under the bed, towels swiped from the shower room and hidden in the washing machine, both boys scurrying round, assessing how the flat would look to their mum.

But it looked better than Melissa thought it would.

"You look good, both of you." She gave them a hug as she laid a hold-all on the floor and sat down on the sofa. "Any ideas about where you want to go for lunch?"

They looked at one another and shrugged.

"Anywhere will be good." Alex still sounded half asleep.

"Are you wondering why I've come?" she asked.

"Not really. Maybe you wanted to see us?" Geoff gave his charming smile.

"I do want to see you. Of course."

"You've an empty nest?" Alex was joking.

"Never when your dad's around. I still have to look after him."

"What then?"

"I'm in Edinburgh for an interview so I thought I'd call in and see you. See if you have any tips."

"An interview?"

"I'm planning to be a student, too."

The boys frowned at each other.

"What do you mean, a student?"

"I've kept the books for your father's business, as you well know. He's now got enough work to keep a full-time book-keeper and I don't want the job."

The boys stared.

"Why not? Dad often says he couldn't have done what he does without you."

"That's true. Now somebody else is going to do it."

The boys had been standing, but now they sat down. Melissa tried to ignore the fact that Geoff had to rescue two beer bottles from his chair in order to do so.

"What are you going to study?"

"Botany." She looked at their uncomprehending faces. "Plants. I'm starting with a course on plant identification at the botanic gardens, then I plan to do a course on herbology, and do some research into the healing properties of herbs."

The boys sat gazing silently at her.

"What brought this on?" Geoff was always the direct one.

"Life."

"I get it," Alex said. "Women go through a phase at your age. You need a good holiday, Mum."

Predictably the boys chose the place that served the best burgers and Melissa managed not to ask if they ever fancied a change of diet. They seemed to have got over their initial surprise.

"I don't suppose you're too old after all," Geoff told her. "We've got mature students in some of our classes. You're becoming a real twentieth-century woman, Mum."

"I've been talking to an old friend. She's giving up her adventurous life to look after a new family. I'm doing things in a different order. It's time for me to branch out before the twenty-first century." Melissa was decisive.

"I suppose it's just you being our mum that makes it strange. What's Dad saying about this?" Alex asked.

"Dad's pleased." Melissa smiled. "Business is doing well and he can get someone else to do all the donkey work."

Melissa had only seen them looking so wary when they had done something wrong. She decided to tease them.

"I'll only be staying in your flat for a couple of days a week," she said, then laughed out loud when she saw the expression on their faces.

"See? You don't want a mum around you all the time. It's time for us all to change, don't you think?" She lifted the bill from the table. "See you at home some time soon. Dad sends his love."

Melissa waved the boys goodbye.

This time she was the one going places. ▪

Broughty Ferry, Dundee

ON the north bank of the silvery Tay lies Broughty Ferry, a former fishing village and popular seaside town.

The settlement grew around the fifteenth-century Broughty Castle, which protected the Tay estuary. The castle now houses a museum of local history, telling the story of the whaling ships that used to depart from Dundee, and of the geology and wildlife in the area.

When the Dundee and Arbroath railway opened in 1838, it encouraged the wealthy mill owners from Dundee to put a little distance between themselves and the noise and grime of the city. Grand villas were built in Broughty Ferry which, at the time, had more millionaires per square mile than any similarly sized town in the country. The railway also made the town more accessible to holidaymakers and Scottish visitors flocked to the "Brighton of the North".

"The Ferry", as it is known locally, is now home to more than 19,000 people. It has become a suburb of Dundee, though it still retains its own distinctive character. ■

Susannah's Secret Service

by Jean Cullop

SUSANNAH regarded the expensive business clothes hanging in her wardrobe. They looked sad and neglected. They were asking to be worn.

Retirement had its plus side, but she missed getting dressed up and setting off for work in the mornings. She had loved her job and she missed it since leaving last year.

Some folk would class her – quite wrongly – as being a retired social worker. Others, not so charitable, looked upon her as a busybody. Neither definition was correct. Her field of work was highly specialised.

In Susannah's own eyes she was a secret agent, slipping unobtrusively into people's lives and serving them just when they most needed her.

Over the years she had helped people of all ages from all backgrounds, but she especially enjoyed meeting elderly folk who had lifetimes of experience to share.

She was looking forward to a talk she was giving to a seniors' club this afternoon. Her talks were not the same as work, but she enjoyed giving them.

Liz, a brusque lady who took the booking over the phone, said that for some folk these meetings were their only outing all week. Despite her manner, Susannah felt Liz was a caring person.

"But it's not right they don't go out," Susannah said to her dressing-table mirror. "People need something to look forward to, no matter how old they are. Never mind, secret agent Susannah is on the way!"

She giggled and scolded herself for talking to her own reflection.

"If you can't talk to yourself at your age, when can you?" the reflection replied.

"I'm not that old!" she snapped back.

That reflection was getting too big for its boots these days.

She concentrated on the day ahead. Sharing knowledge about her herbs was a joy for Susannah. She had one talk about herbs in vegetables and salads, one on herbs for health, and her personal favourite, "Herbs In Cooking", which she was giving today. Seniors enjoyed that one even if they no longer prepared their own meals.

She never thought of herself as being old.

Illustration by Kirk Houston.

"I wonder why that is?" she mused.

"It's only because you keep active," her reflection replied. "If you had aching bones and wonky knees you might think differently."

The mirror image seemed to have a mind of its own and needed taking down a peg or two, but today she was far too busy to worry about that.

Instead she gathered together the items she would need for this afternoon, then she made some lavender scones. They always went down well. Few people even considered using lavender in cooking, but edible lavender was delicious.

She potted out some parsley to be grown on kitchen window-sills. She would give those as gifts.

Susannah's modern bungalow was surrounded on three sides by an old-fashioned cottage garden, and despite the poor soil, everything she planted flourished.

It had puzzled her husband, because dear Charles had had no success at all with their poor soil. But he had been gone these 20 years. He never once guessed the secret of Susannah's success.

Since his death, Susannah had lived alone, their not having been blessed with children, but alone didn't have to mean lonely. She was too busy for that! Though she did miss going to work.

Later that day, in the bright but badly in need of updating hall, Susannah cast her eye over her waiting audience, deciding what she thought they would most like to hear.

How times had changed! Gone were the cauliflower perms, wrinkled Nora Batty stockings and tweed skirts associated with the over-sixties. These ladies sported neat coiffures and wore smart trousers and tops, much like the cheerful red outfit she was wearing today.

Most were chatting, although one person seemed to keep herself to herself, another was intent on rearranging the chairs and telling others where to sit, and someone on the front row was fast asleep.

The atmosphere was very relaxed. Folk seemed to be accepted for who they were. Liz, the lady who had taken the booking, winked at Susannah.

"Ethel nods off every week then says how much she enjoyed the talk. If she snores too loudly Maud gives her a gentle prod."

Susannah giggled. She had been right about Liz. Her care for the folk who came to the club was evident from her manner, bringing with it a pleasant aura.

Susannah was good with auras. It went with her secret service job.

Rather like a sports teacher organising a game of hockey, Liz blew a whistle for attention. The hall was instantly silent. The lady organising the chairs sat down and Susannah was introduced as an expert in all things herbal.

Susannah worked through her notes, but really she knew them off by heart. She never kept to the script, instead tailoring the talk to her audience's needs – not counting those who were actually asleep, of course.

Herbs in cooking always went down well, as would her lavender scones at teatime. They were familiar, but different enough to be interesting.

This was a jolly bunch and when the talk ended they asked several questions, apart from that lady who was sitting by herself. She wasn't dressed so smartly as the others and something about her niggled Susannah.

Perhaps this lady was painfully shy, or perhaps she just preferred her own company to making small talk. If so, why come to a gathering such as this?

Before she had a chance to find out, the lady was whisked away by a young man who arrived to take her home.

"Her name is Ada Finch and that's her grandson," Liz explained later. "Sadly her son and daughter-in-law were involved in a fatal car crash and the grandson is all she has in her family."

"That is so sad!" Susannah exclaimed.

"We've all tried to help her to no avail. Different organisations for the elderly have approached her, but she really doesn't want to know. She's been coming here for some years and I think it's because we are familiar to her. She lives in that cottage by the ring road."

Susannah knew the house, which could at best be described as dilapidated.

Maybe Ada Finch simply didn't take to new ideas and gatherings, but she could be struggling with grief. We were all different.

Her heart missed a beat. Ada had left before she had time for tea, and who could resist a lavender scone?

Something told Susannah that this could well be a time to bring her secret service out of retirement. The situation was desperate and the date was perfect.

∗   ∗   ∗   ∗

By the time she got home Susannah's head was buzzing with ideas. She hadn't been this inspired since finishing work.

She packed some lavender scones in a plastic box – Ada had missed hers by leaving early. Then she took a cutting from her edible lavender and planted it in a pretty pot. That done, she found her reference book. It always helped.

But by six o'clock she had found nothing suitable and wondered if Ada deserved better than words from a dusty book.

Frowning, she heated some soup to get her brain cells working, but by six o'clock she still had no idea how to help Ada. Her cat, Mog, rubbed against her legs to tell her he was hungry and lonely.

"That's it," she cried, terrifying the cat, who screeched. He was getting too old for these outbursts. "Ada Finch is lonely! She needs a friend."

Mog stared balefully.

"It's all right for you, Mog! You have me and I have you. Ada has nobody. You want me to help her, don't you?"

The cat squawked, stalked off and then flopped down on top of the radiator. Well, he would just have to stay there for now. She would make it up to him when she came home from work.

Home from work . . . The very sound of the words was exciting. And if she had to come out of retirement, what better day than today?

Having made sure she had everything she needed, Susannah jotted down the recipe for lavender scones, then took out her favourite set of work clothes: black with a scarlet lining.

She hesitated. The satin cape and chic pointed hat didn't seem suitable for this visit. It was company Ada needed, not fancy clothes and an old book of spells.

Susannah resolved that this would not be a one-off call, either; she knew the importance of commitment.

She had picked up a leaflet on helping the elderly before she had left the meeting hall. It looked promising. You had to give a tea party once a month. She could make her lavender scones!

She retrieved her car keys from Mog's bed. How on earth did they get there?

She knew the ring road would be busy at this time of day. Her besom stood by the front door. Ada would never know what mode of transport she used. Surely it wouldn't hurt to take it out of retirement for one night? It was such a convenient way to travel.

The black cat purred and jumped on board. After all, it *was* Hallowe'en. ∎

Richard Burton

Photoshot.

IT'S sometimes difficult to believe that from his humble origins – born the son of a coalminer in November 1925 in a tiny Welsh village – Richard Walter Jenkins would become Richard Burton, the Hollywood legend.

This versatile actor worked on the stage, screen, TV and radio, enjoying a career that spanned decades.

He earned seven Oscar nominations for his work in the likes of "The Robe" and "Who's Afraid Of Virginia Woolf?", starring alongside Elizabeth Taylor. The pair worked in 11 films together, their first being "Cleopatra", in which Burton played Mark Antony.

Burton went on to act in more than 40 films, most notably "Look Back In Anger", "Anne Of The Thousand Days", "The Spy Who Came In From The Cold" and "Equus".

Who would have believed that from such humble beginnings Burton would leave such a lasting mark as one of Hollywood's greats? ■

Illustration by iStock.

The Light In The Sky

by Rebecca Mansell

R EMEMBER, remember, the fifth of November . . .

Actually, it was a date that Julia wished with all her heart that she didn't have to remember. It had been a cold and dark day last year when she rang the hospital to check on her father's progress. He'd been admitted a week before because of a chest infection.

Every day she visited, and he seemed to be improving.

"I keep forgetting the rules the hospital has about flowers," she'd said cheerfully that day. "I was thinking of bringing some in when I see him later."

"Mrs Evans." The nurse spoke gently and with hesitancy.

Immediately, Julia felt a strange coldness spread throughout her body.

"What is it?"

"You ought to come in to the hospital," the nurse had responded calmly, but Julia knew. She just knew.

On the fifth of November her father passed away.

While other families were outside enjoying fireworks and warming themselves next to bonfires, Julia stayed in. Sitting on the sofa, cuddling her trembling cocker spaniel, Bingo – who hated the bangs he could hear outside – she remembered days gone by and she grieved for the loss of her father.

Jake took the children to the local fireworks display to distract them, but they returned looking forlorn and lost. They loved their grandpa very much.

*   *   *   *

"I don't know where the year has gone." Julia sighed into her coffee mug.

It was the morning of the fourth of November. The day had dawned bright and crisp but her mind was full of memories. She glanced up at her husband.

"Apart from last year, we've always had our very own fireworks display."

Jake sat down beside her and took her cool hands in his large, warm ones.

"You don't want to do that this year?"

"It feels too early." Julia's large green eyes were troubled. "But Cathy and Lucas are only ten and twelve. It seems wrong for them to miss out."

Jake kissed his wife gently on her forehead.

"They're young, but they will understand. They still miss their grandpa."

From when the kids could walk, they'd spent every weekend with their grandpa. At first it was to play games in the garden, running around the little maze he had created especially for them, the bushes cut to just the right height. His garden had been a magical wonderland for them.

Then, as they got older, he helped them with their homework and read fascinating adventure stories from old, scribbled notebooks. The children would come home full of tales of all that Grandpa had done.

Now, Cathy spent her time with her best friend, Della, cooped up in her bedroom each weekend. And Lucas just read. He was halfway through "Huckleberry Finn" after finishing "Robinson Crusoe".

Jake paused and looked at Julia thoughtfully.

"Is this what your father would have wanted?"

Julia frowned. Her father had loved Bonfire Night. She was sure it had been his light-heartedness that kept him going after her mother had passed away five years before. He'd always known how to keep his inner child having fun.

Julia's own childlike playfulness seemed to have vanished.

She pushed her hair from her tired eyes.

"It's not as if the kids have mentioned anything, is it?"

At that moment, they were interrupted by a couple of giggling girls rushing into the kitchen.

"Mum, Dad!" Cathy's eyes were alight with excitement. "We will be having fireworks in the back garden this year, won't we?"

Julia raised her eyebrows to Jake.

"Well . . ." He hesitated.

"Oh, please, Daddy!" Cathy grabbed his hands and swung around him happily, just like she used to before their world had turned upside-down. "Della wants to come, and we used to have such amazing fireworks."

Julia looked at her daughter with surprise. It had been a while since she'd seen her so full of life.

"Sweetheart, we weren't really planning on having our own display, and Bonfire Night is tomorrow. There isn't time."

Julia and Jake shared a look once they saw Cathy's disappointed expression.

"What's happening?" Lucas mumbled as he strolled into the kitchen, his dark fringe covering his eyes.

"It's about what isn't happening," Cathy replied, rolling her eyes at her best friend.

"Eh?" Lucas was trying to read "Huckleberry Finn" and open the fridge door at the same time.

"Put the book down." Jake laughed. "It will still be there after you've got your drink from the fridge!"

"Yes, Dad," Lucas muttered. "What's not happening?"

"Just our fireworks display." Cathy sighed dramatically. "Della wanted to come."

"You've got the sensitivity of a mole rat," her brother said, glaring at her from beneath his mop of hair.

"A what?" Cathy asked. "What is a mole rat?"

"It lives underground in East Africa and doesn't feel the pain of acid."

Cathy folded her arms petulantly and waited for her brother to explain further.

Lucas took a swig of his drink, glanced at his parents and then back at his sister.

"Grandpa died last year on Bonfire Night, or have you forgotten?"

Cathy looked down at her feet.

"I know that," she whispered. "It's just that, well, I thought . . ."

"That's the problem," Lucas said, picking up his book. "You don't think. Well, you do, but only of yourself and no-one else."

"Now, son." Jake spoke with a warning tone.

Cathy looked upset and Lucas, who rarely showed emotion, was becoming more incensed by the argument.

Julia suddenly rose to her feet.

"I know you both miss your grandpa very much," she said quietly. "Cathy, I realise you just want to have fun and remember him that way."

Cathy nodded her head with a small smile.

"And Lucas, I understand you want to preserve his memory and you are thinking of us, too. Thank you."

Lucas remained quiet but Julia could see the tears in his eyes.

"What do you want, Mum?"

Julia looked down into her daughter's blue eyes and felt a lump in her throat.

"Well." Her voice trembled a little. "That's the problem. I don't know."

The next moment the kitchen door swung open and the final member of the family arrived.

Bingo trotted towards Julia and sat down in front of her with his head on one side. Then he padded towards the door to the garden and back again, looking at her beseechingly.

Julia smiled.

"But I do know one thing. Bingo needs a walk. Who wants to take him?"

As the children argued over whose turn it was, Della cuddled the dog affectionately. Julia's eyes met with Jake's again and he smiled at her reassuringly.

There was something else that Julia knew. Despite everything, despite Bonfire Night, despite all those glorious fireworks that were bound to light up the sky tomorrow night, life still went on.

*　　*　　*　　*

What Julia loved most about their house was the swing in the garden. She'd always wanted one as a child. So when Julia and Jake picked this house she was delighted to find an old rusty swing in the garden.

It wasn't long before Jake made it presentable and safe, and many a time Julia sat upon it to relax.

The children loved it, too, but it was really Julia who found the most comfort in it. Just like she was doing now.

It was the evening of the fourth of November. The kids were in bed, Jake was tinkering with his car in the garage and Julia had nothing else to do but sit and think.

She swung gently back and forth on the swing, not even feeling the coolness of the night. She recalled days gone by: happy times with her parents and her father's contagious laugh.

She missed him so very much.

Suddenly a strange whizzing sound alerted her and then she almost jumped out of her skin when a loud bang seemed to make the ground beneath her feet vibrate.

Looking up, the night sky seemed to erupt into a rainbow of colours, just like stars falling to the earth.

Julia gazed at the fireworks with awe. Obviously someone couldn't wait for tomorrow night.

Then, as quickly as the display had started, it ended, and Julia decided to go inside for a mug of hot chocolate.

"Let off a firework just for me."

Julia caught her breath. Slowly she rose from the swing and turned around. There was no-one there, and yet she had distinctly heard a voice.

And it had sounded just like her father . . .

*　*　*　*

"Where have you been?" Jake asked the following morning, his face full of concern. "I was worried when I got up and found you weren't here."

Julia beamed at him.

"I went out to get these."

In the hallway were boxes and boxes of fireworks. There were rockets, Roman candles, a Catherine wheel and fountains.

"Wow!" he said, looking at his wife's flushed face. "Did you buy every firework the town has in stock?"

"Almost." Julia looked tired but happy. "Something told me last night that Dad would want us to celebrate this year. That all would be fine."

Suddenly Jake and Julia realised the kids were behind them, rubbing their bleary eyes.

"So, what do you think?" Julia asked them, smiling.

"I think it will be fantastic!" Cathy hugged her mother.

"The neighbours will love it, too," Lucas said in awe. "Wow, Mum, this firework is huge! What does it do?"

"That one is called the Light In The Sky and it really does what it says on the box – brightens up the whole sky."

"I can't wait to see that one." Lucas grinned, flicking back his hair from his face.

"Do you think Grandpa will be able to see it from heaven, if it's that bright?" Cathy gazed up at her mother.

Julia smiled down at her. She knew then, with certainty, that she'd done the right thing.

"Oh, yes," she replied. "I think so. That one we will light especially for Grandpa. We'll let off a firework just for him."

That night a bright firework lit up the entire night sky. It could be seen all over town.

Within all the cheers and gasps of amazement, Julia swore she could hear laughter.

And she knew, in her heart, her father was with them, enjoying the display and laughing at the adventure of it all. Though no firework could match him, for he was the true light in the sky . . . ■

Church Stretton, Shropshire

IN the south Shropshire hills, on the English/Welsh border, the historic market town of Church Stretton occupies a spot that has been inhabited for thousands of years. Nearby Caer Caradoc, overlooking the town, is the site of an Iron Age hill fort.

In 1214 the town was already thriving. King John granted a charter in that year for a weekly market. A market is still held in the town every Thursday, and it takes place in the square, which has been in use since the 13th century.

The beautiful countryside around the town was an inspiration for poets and authors and features in the work of A.E. Houseman, Mary Webb and children's author Malcolm Saville. The author Hesba Stretton lived here for a time. In St Laurence's Church there is a plaque to her memory, as well as a stained-glass window featuring the character of Jessica from her story "Jessica's First Prayer". ∎

Illustration by Mandy Dixon.

Rose Mantle

by Louise McIvor

EVERYONE told them they were crazy to be looking for a house. "Stay in your lovely apartment," Jenna's mum said. "The rent is reasonable and it's near your jobs. Give yourselves another few years before you even think of such an investment."

"Matthew and I have both fallen in love with Rose Mantle," Jenna said, sipping her latte. "As soon as I saw the house online I just thought it would make a great family home. We're viewing it tomorrow."

"Well, you know that your father and I will help in any way we can," her mum said, clearly aware that once Jenna put her mind to something, there was no stopping her.

What Jenna didn't tell her mother was that Rose Mantle had seen better days. Even in its photograph it looked rather forlorn and unloved, with a garden that had not seen a lawnmower in many a year and chipped paint on the window-frames. The fact that the website didn't even feature any interior photos spoke volumes.

The house was also just over their budget, but Matthew said one reason he had married Jenna was that she was good at seeing the potential in things.

"Look at me – I didn't create a good first impression, yet you married me," he teased, reminding Jenna of their first date when he had forgotten his wallet and spilled red wine over her pale linen dress.

"I know a good thing when I see it," Jenna teased back.

"Seriously, Jenna, you do. It does say 'Some updating required', which is estate agent language for 'Needs a lot of work'. Let's do a viewing and take things from there. Our lease is up on this place next month anyway."

Matthew didn't need to add that they hadn't been able to afford all the smart houses in the new developments that they had viewed.

"But you're so busy," Jenna said.

Matthew was in his second year as a qualified solicitor and was lucky if he was able to finish by six p.m. on a Friday.

Jenna's hours were more flexible. She worked for a local college, updating the website and putting together the college's newsletter among numerous other things.

Over the past year Jenna and Matthew had been saving like mad to afford a deposit. Whether it would be enough was anyone's guess.

Jenna turned back to the few photos that were on the website.

"Look, I'll bet there's a good driveway beneath those thistles sprouting through the paving slabs," she said. "And if the basic structure is sound we can update as we go along. I'm not the sort of girl who demands an en-suite bathroom and a TV in the shower."

They'd laughed when they had seen this very thing in one of the DIY stores in town.

"You sort out a time that suits you, Jenna," Matthew said. "If I can't make it, we can always arrange a second viewing."

*   *   *   *

The *For Sale* sign was partially hidden behind an overgrown hydrangea bush. It was a rainy day and blowing a gale so strong that Jenna's umbrella flew inside out as soon as she got out of the car.

She peered through the single-glazed windows with their rotting frames and could see that the rooms were well proportioned. She guessed that the front would get the sun after lunch every day.

She could also see, when the estate agent eventually got the front door open through the mound of take-away food menus, that there was a beautiful wooden floor underneath the dust.

"How long has it been on the market?" Jenna asked.

"Over a year," the estate agent said. "As you can see, it's redbrick and the basic property is a good one underneath the rather dated décor."

The estate agent waved his hand vaguely at the swirly patterned carpet.

"I'd like to take a good look around," Jenna said.

"Take your time. I've grown rather fond of the old house. The previous owner died and her son lives in Canada, so of course he wants to sell, but frankly, he doesn't want the bother of spending any money on it. The thing is, with a new bathroom, kitchen and double glazing, you'd have a knockout property. And the new houses they're putting up don't have half the space of these older ones."

It was refreshing to have such candour. It was still raining and there didn't appear to be any heating on but there was no smell of damp.

Rose Mantle. What a lovely name, Jenna thought.

The kitchen had 1980s melamine units with ugly metal ridges for handles. There was a big gap where the washing machine had been.

The bathroom was a riot of pale pink and grey, and the bathroom suite had an old-fashioned shower hooked up to the bath taps.

The master bedroom had white built-in units taking up one wall. Jenna took out her tape measure. She calculated that if they removed the units and just put in a wardrobe, this room would be considerably bigger than most of the rooms in the new townhouses.

The other two bedrooms were similarly proportioned and they could perhaps use one as a home office, or –

"What do you think?" the estate agent said.

It was a Friday afternoon and the poor man was possibly as anxious as she was to go home and sink on to the sofa.

"I'd like to arrange a time when my husband's free to view the house, too," Jenna said, not wanting to give too much away without Matthew there.

"We can do that, no bother. There are no offers yet," the estate agent said.

∗   ∗   ∗   ∗

As soon as Matthew saw Rose Mantle his reaction was the same as Jenna's.

"There's a lovely back garden as well," he said, seeing it through Jenna's eyes – past the rusting metal swing frame and past the knee-high grass which all but obliterated the flower-beds.

"You do remember that I can hardly bang in a nail?" he warned.

"But you can hold the ladder while I do!" Jenna laughed, giving Matthew a hug.

Their friends said that was why they were so well matched. Matthew could figure out any legal problem within minutes.

It was Jenna who would read the instructions on self-assembly furniture, neatly laying out each screw, rod and piece. Matthew would act as "gaffer's mate", holding pieces together and fetching things from Jenna's toolbox.

It was Jenna who knew that a room could be transformed by a coat of emulsion and that a good roller and dust sheets were a girl's best friend.

The only thing Jenna wouldn't attempt were electrics, but Matthew had an uncle who was a retired electrician so they could always call on him.

"It's the space I like. The apartment is just too small," Jenna said.

"Think what this place would be like on a nice summer's afternoon."

"Enough room for a picnic table and chairs!"

"And a barbecue! It's right at the edge of our budget, though," he whispered while the estate agent was taking a call on his mobile. "I think we should go home and think about this over some prawn crackers and egg fried rice!"

So Jenna and Matthew sat down that evening and worked everything out over their Chinese food. Matthew took the figure the mortgage advisor had given them as a guideline, but they would also have to factor in repairs.

Jenna made a list of everything they would need to do to the house. The list was long.

"The kitchen and bathroom will need to be done. There's no central heating, just some ancient storage heaters. We would need double glazing straight off, to say nothing of decorating. And we're going to need your uncle sooner rather than later."

"Furniture . . ." Matthew added.

"We could get everyone to raid their attics, and there are always the charity shops," Jenna said, adding that to her list.

"We'd obviously get a full survey done," Matthew said. "But as long as the basic structure of the house is sound, I think we should just go ahead. We won't have any wiggle room on this figure, though."

Buoyed up by optimism, Jenna was already furnishing the rooms in her mind, working out colour schemes and picturing herself hanging out washing in that big garden, rather than having to shove it into the tumble dryer in the tiny apartment.

After another appointment with their mortgage advisor, they took a deep breath, phoned the estate agent and put in their offer.

The offer was promptly rejected.

Jenna, who was fielding phone calls from the estate agent that day as Matthew was in court, didn't know what to do.

On the bus on the way home from work she felt sick and anxious, realising that all her fantasies about Rose Mantle might never come to fruition.

"We can't go any higher," Matthew said when he got home that night. "You know what the mortgage advisor said. We're already stretching it."

"It's just hard. We really did have our hearts set on Rose Mantle. But I know you're right," Jenna said, barely able to speak.

Matthew gave her a hug and then hit the number of the Chinese take-away on his phone.

"There's no point in thinking too much more while we're tired and hungry, darling," he added.

Afterwards, they resigned themselves to looking at other properties. However, in bed that evening, Jenna kept thinking of the name of the Chinese take-away: "Good Luck".

We could do with a little more of that, she thought, finally falling asleep and dreaming of swinging on the swing at Rose Mantle on a sunny summer's day.

*   *   *   *

They viewed five more properties. None had cracked window-frames or knee-high grass. One even had a snazzy en-suite bathroom in the master bedroom and another one had a new kitchen.

If Jenna were being honest with herself, if the estate agent had offered her Buckingham Palace at a knockdown price, she would have found some fault, because it wouldn't have been Rose Mantle.

But push on they must. Not only was their lease on the apartment coming to an end, but Jenna had an extra reason to want to be in a new home.

She had recently found out that she was expecting and had been through a rollercoaster of emotions in the last few weeks. Delight at being pregnant; anxiety at them taking on a mortgage with a baby on the way and all the other things – like looking at every young mother with a baby buggy and assuming that she couldn't possibly do it. That she'd be found wanting.

Still, the Rose Mantle dreams persisted. One night, Jenna dreamed she was vacuuming the house's swirly patterned carpet, and in another dream, she was trying to put up a shelf that kept falling down.

*   *   *   *

The lease on their flat had ended and Matthew and Jenna were staying with Jenna's parents, which seemed to be the best thing as they didn't want to commit to another six-month lease.

Although part of Jenna loved being with her parents, she felt tired and out of sorts, coping with morning sickness and longing for her own space.

That Saturday morning Matthew and Jenna were viewing a new-build townhouse. Jenna had resigned herself to putting all thoughts of Rose Mantle from her head.

Jenna realised that the townhouse ticked all the right boxes.

"There's good parking and the garden's OK," Matthew said dully.

"The rooms are smaller than Rose Mantle, but that's true of most of the new builds we've seen, and I like the kitchen diner," Jenna agreed.

"We wouldn't need to do anything to it. And it's smaller than some of the other houses, therefore more affordable."

"I know," Jenna said sadly.

"That's why we call these townhouses 'turnkey'," the estate agent said.

"You can just move straight in."

Just then, the agent's mobile rang, leaving Jenna and Matthew to discuss things a little more freely.

"It's within our price range," Jenna said. "Mum and Dad have been so kind, but we can't stay with them for ever."

"Tell you what, let's go home and think about it over the weekend. Chinese OK? I think your mum and dad are out at their church AGM tonight," Matthew said.

On Monday morning Jenna's mobile rang just as she was about to phone the estate agent with their offer on the townhouse. She looked at the screen and swiped the green answer button.

"I was just going to call you," Jenna said.

"I've news for you two," the estate agent said. "Are you still interested in Rose Mantle? I had an e-mail from Canada over the weekend. The vendor's finally seen sense and decided to lower the asking price."

Jenna scribbled down the new asking price. It wasn't a huge drop but she was too excited that Rose Mantle was once again available to think straight.

Matthew was in court again that day so she had to be content with texting him, promising to get back to the estate agent as soon as she could.

It was lunchtime before her mobile pinged.

Offer the asking price. It's within our price range now.

Jenna phoned the estate agent.

∗　　∗　　∗　　∗

When they finally got the key to Rose Mantle it was a Friday afternoon. It was again blowing a gale and lashing with rain.

However, even the grumpy removal van driver who had phoned to say he'd be an hour late couldn't dampen Jenna's sunny mood.

Matthew had an important case so couldn't take any extra time off work, so it had been up to Jenna to see the solicitor and the lady at the bank, and finally to pick up the keys from the estate agent.

The door still stuck on the mound of take-away leaflets behind the door. Jenna looked out at the rain teeming down on the overgrown garden and felt a rush of happiness. She looked at her watch to see what was keeping Matthew.

She heard a sound and then realised that it was the old-fashioned doorbell. In their house, their very own house.

It was Matthew, with a bunch of yellow roses.

"Roses in Rose Mantle!"

Jenna took the roses and put them down on the kitchen bench.

"It's beautiful, isn't it?"

Matthew hugged his resourceful wife.

"Yes, darling, it is." ∎

Doris Day

Photoshot.

BORN Doris Mary Ann von Kappelhoff in April 1924 in Ohio, this actress started her career as a big band singer in 1939.

Before this, she studied ballet and tap dance while growing up, and it wasn't until a leg injury in her teens forced her to change direction that she turned her attention to singing.

With her voice and looks, it was little wonder that she made it big in musicals, and she rose to the challenge in her film debut "Romance On The High Seas" in 1948. However, Day could also turn her hand to more dramatic roles and played alongside Kirk Douglas in "Young Man With A Horn".

Her role in "Calamity Jane" is fondly remembered, as is her trademark tune "Que Sera, Sera", from the thriller "The Man Who Knew Too Much", which was directed by Alfred Hitchcock.

One of the best-loved actresses of the era, Day enjoyed a box-office hit with the film adaptation of the popular musical "The Pajama Game" and two years later followed this with another smash hit, "Pillow Talk", in which she teamed up with Rock Hudson.

Day then switched her attention to television with "The Doris Day Show", which ran from 1968 to 1973. ■

The Fireside Club

by H. Johnson-Mack

THE night was bitterly cold, the snowy midwinter landscape looking like a scene straight out of a Dickens novel. Leaning gloved hands on her stick, Bridie let her breath out on a cloud, gazing beyond the small community of barn conversions to the silent, white countryside beyond. There was a stark beauty to it, but still Bridie shivered and turned gratefully towards the glow of the largest barn, where she was bound.

Her host, Roger, met her at the door, his snowy hair perfectly suited to the season and his smile welcoming as he drew her inside.

"Come in, dear heart. I've saved you the best spot by the fire."

Bridie allowed him to ease her out of her coat. Always the gentleman, Roger. Perhaps because he was the architect who'd created the little community of Beeches Brook Farm, he seemed to feel accountable to its residents.

Not that Bridie minded. Though she'd chosen this spot for its rural tranquillity, at her age and especially at this time of year she liked to know there were considerate neighbours nearby. But whether the folk in tonight's particular gathering would appreciate Roger's efforts remained to be seen.

"Mulled wine, or hot spiced apple cup?"

"Wine, please, Roger. You may never drink the stuff yourself, but you certainly buy the best for the rest of us!"

Flinging her scarf on to the hat stand, Bridie moved to greet the other guests – Roger's great-nephew, Jack, also an architect, and Fleur, the fairy-like tapestry artist who had the smallest of the three properties on site, adjoining Bridie's.

"Hello, my darlings. Don't you just love Roger's answer to a wintry night in?" Jack raised his brows.

"That depends on what exactly he has planned."

"Oh, just a bit of fun by the fireside." Roger winked at Bridie as he stooped to offer her a steaming tankard.

Bridie sniffed appreciatively, then wrapped her hands around the mug.

"Nothing too physical, I hope. My knees get really cranky in this weather."

"He did say it was a game," Jack warned as he tucked a footstool under her ankles and handed Fleur, on the rug, a huge floor cushion to lean back on.

Roger's eyes twinkled.

"Don't worry. It's no more than a mind game. And there's a prize, by the way, for guessing correctly."

He settled into the wing chair opposite Bridie and for a while talk was general

Illustration by iStock.

as they all sipped their steaming drinks. As usual, Fleur spoke little, as is the way of those afflicted with social anxiety. But at least she was here, and Bridie, seeing Fleur's cheeks aglow with healthy colour, began to relax.

Perhaps their host was right in his assessment of the shy young woman – that what she needed most was a safe environment in which to gain confidence. She could surely then make the most of her life, as she deserved to be able to do.

"Now that we're all warm," Roger announced after a while, his weathered features reflecting the bobbing firelight, "I am going to tell you a tale."

Bridie rubbed her hands together.

"Oh, good! I love stories."

*   *   *   *

From her position on the floor, Fleur smiled at the older woman's enthusiasm. With a personality as vibrant as her ever-changing hair colour, Bridie managed to be friendly and fun but never intrusive, exactly the kind of person that Fleur

161

needed in her life. It wasn't easy for an introvert like herself to socialise, so it was nice to have neighbours like Bridie and the gallant Roger so close by.

Since moving to the serene setting of Beeches Brook, Fleur's creativity levels had soared and her nerves lessened, and she'd begun to believe she really could make a successful living from her loom, doing what she loved.

She returned her attention to Roger as he began his tale.

"Once upon a time there lived a solitary man. He never went out for weeks at a time; never had visitors. One day, he closed all the windows, turned off all the lights and left the building."

Fingers steepled, Roger leaned forward and gazed solemnly round the circle.

"That action was to endanger the lives of six people. Why?"

Fleur's brows drew together as she considered Roger's tale. Bridie emitted one of her throaty chuckles.

"Wow. That's quite a riddle."

Roger smiled, readily obliging when Jack asked, "Tell it again, would you?"

Fleur listened more carefully this time, noting Jack's resolute expression as Roger spoke.

She'd only met Jack once or twice. He came across as a nice guy but with a wicked sense of humour. In his face she saw that determination that had led his great-uncle to the top of his trade. Jack wanted to be the one to solve this riddle.

Fleur had no idea that, along with that thought, she herself had sat up and straightened her shoulders.

"The man's a hermit," Jack was saying now. "That's why he lives alone."

Fleur cleared her throat, pushing past her timidity to speak.

"Why would a hermit represent harm to others?"

Jack looked thrown. Bridie tapped her chair arm in a thoughtful rhythm.

"His profession's significant, I think," she mused.

Jack chewed absently on a thumbnail.

"I agree. Perhaps he's a spy, or some kind of assassin."

Fleur raised her brows.

"All spies live alone? That's a pretty broad assumption."

Jack's look in her direction was wide-eyed, as if pleasantly surprised by her insight, and more, by her speaking it aloud so assuredly. He slowly grinned.

Fleur flushed, and after a moment, she lowered her gaze.

The barn fell quiet as the guests continued to ponder. Smiling to himself, Roger rose and disappeared into the kitchen. It was time for more wine.

*   *   *   *

As Jack's mind turned over the riddle, his eyes wandered round the handsome mix of historic cosiness and modern convenience that his great-uncle had created in this 17th-century barn.

It was a style he'd tried to emulate, content to be guided in his career by a man who was as humble as he was gifted. He'd only known Roger since he was at college, really; before that, Roger had been pretty solitary.

Now in his later years and with Jack to carry his creations on into the next generation, Roger had the time to indulge in other pleasures besides his architectural work. Like hosting these little get-togethers and driving his guests crazy with a puzzle that they just couldn't solve!

"OK," he conceded at last. "So we're not sure who the man is. Then what about where he lives?"

"Yes." Bridie offered her glass for Roger to refill, amused by the delight in his face that the group were so absorbed in his game. "The building."

"Somewhere he can't leave unattended, perhaps," Jack said.

Then he blinked at the blinding smile Fleur sent him.

"I think you might be on to something there," she murmured.

She was playing with her ponytail, having fallen back into her habitual silence.

Jack watched her with a dawning wonder, noting the fine, long fingers entwined in her buttermilk hair and the soft, pensive eyes as she stared reflectively at the flames in the hearth.

He shook himself. Focus, Jack!

He ticked off what he considered the riddle's important points on his fingers.

"OK, then. Lives alone; has no visitors; turned off the lights and endangered lives when leaving the building."

Gasping, Fleur rose up on her knees.

"I think I've got it!" she cried, half in disbelief. "I think I know the answer!"

"What?" the others demanded in unison.

"'Turned off the lights and left'," Fleur repeated. "Where else can you think of where that would be a danger, but a lighthouse? He's a lighthouse keeper!"

There was a pause.

"Of course!" everyone erupted.

Roger applauded, looking pleased as punch.

"Well done, my young nymph. You are correct."

"Yes, well done," Jack echoed. "You're not just a pretty face, are you?"

Like a startled fawn, Fleur ducked her head and looked ready to bolt from the room. Jack remembered his uncle saying that she suffered from acute shyness.

He half-rose to go to her, but Roger had lifted an old hurricane lamp from the mantelpiece and was gently holding it out to her.

"Here's your prize. A lantern from my old Keeper's Cottage."

"Oh, I couldn't!" Fleur protested, blushing. "It's so beautiful."

Roger agreed.

"Perfect for hanging above our resident artist's studio door. Please take it. It would make me very happy to see it shining there."

After another hesitation, Fleur bashfully accepted the little square lantern, delighting in the way the firelight caught the lead-faceted glass.

"You've inspired me," she murmured, her gaze distant. "I've images in my mind of a lighthouse, a swinging lantern and a boat being tossed about on the waves. I think I'll see if I can weave it into a tapestry design, with a rich palette of green and blue. 'On Stormy Seas', I might call it."

"So, what's the next challenge?" Bridie wondered after a moment.

Roger smiled.

"How much chocolate mud pie you can eat?"

Bridie blinked.

"Oh, right. I was thinking of Scrabble."

∗　∗　∗　∗

It had been a lovely night, Bridie reflected as once more she faced the white, silent world outside.

"I think I'll ask Unc to make this a regular event," Jack mused as he escorted the ladies on the short walk home.

After a moment, Fleur shyly agreed.

"It needs a name, though. Something quaint, like 'The Fireside Club'."

"The Fireside Club," Bridie echoed. "I like the sound of that. I wonder what Roger will think up for us next time? Well, goodnight, my dears. Take care on that ice by Fleur's studio. It's a little slippy."

She almost laughed out loud as she watched Jack guiding Fleur's steps round the side of the barn, keeping hold of her for much longer than the small ice patch merited.

Roger's plan for helping Fleur overcome her social issues might have succeeded a little too well, she thought, for there was a blossoming romance if ever she saw one!

∗　∗　∗　∗

From his doorway, Roger watched until his guests were out of sight, then let his gaze drift over the white world beyond Beeches Brook.

Tonight had gone even better than he'd hoped. Fleur was on her way to beating her social insecurities, and, finally, he himself had been able to lay to rest the ghost of his past in a most strange but satisfying way.

That incredibly irresponsible wild night when, drunk on duty, he had almost caused the deaths of an off-course trawler crew, had haunted Roger for decades. He had never been back to a lighthouse since that night, had never again let down his guard nor touched one drop of alcohol.

Now, at last, he felt free.

If the lovely Fleur ever did create that seascape tapestry, he would buy it and give it pride of place above his hearth. He could trust her to keep the lighthouse lantern burning so that from now on, all those within reach of its light could sleep soundly in their beds, for ever safe from storms . . . ∎

Rock Hudson

Photoshot.

BORN Roy Harold Scherer Jr in November 1925 in Illinois, Rock Hudson was always going to look good on the big screen. When he moved to Hollywood in a bid to become an actor, he first had to work as a truck driver and spent a lot of his time hanging around the film studios in the hope of being discovered.

Hudson was a charismatic man and very charming, so it wasn't long before he got the break he desired.

However, looks aside, critics acknowledged he had a talent for acting, which was clearly evident when he starred in "Giant" alongside Elizabeth Taylor and James Dean.

He's fondly remembered for his romantic roles in "Pillow Talk", alongside Doris Day, and "Lover Come Back".

If you've ever wondered where he got his name from, apparently a talent scout gave him the moniker "Rock" after the Rock of Gibraltar, and "Hudson" for the Hudson River.

In later life he branched out into television, appearing in "McMillan & Wife" and "Dynasty".

Despite having had no professional training as an actor, Rock Hudson still managed to make his mark and his talents are recognised to this day. ■

165

A Creative Christmas

by Isobel J. Sayer

TANYA paused from her concentration as she worked out their accounts. She glanced up at Henry, who was avidly watching a football match on the television. She nearly started talking to him about their finances, but decided not to interrupt his attention from the game in front of him.

Turning back to her trusty book with its neatly filled-out columns, she looked at the figures in front of her. The essentials were covered for the next few months. Even if her husband's maintenance business didn't pick up until the weather improved, they could manage the rent, bills and food on her wages.

She was about to start a tentative conversation about Christmas when a joyful whoop came from her left. His team had obviously just scored.

Tanya smiled to herself, as she looked lovingly at her husband of five years sitting on the edge of the sofa, cheering his team on.

As if he knew she was watching him, he turned to her, then glanced up at the ceiling.

"Sorry," he whispered.

She smiled at him. If the loud cheer just now hadn't woken their son, then talking at normal volume probably wouldn't.

"I'll go and check on him," she reassured him, leaving her notebook with its neat pencilled rows of figures open on the coffee table.

She peered in through the darkened bedroom doorway, her eyes adjusting to the silhouetted form of their nine-month-old baby, lying prostrate on his back, just visible from the hall light.

She tiptoed in and he stirred and sucked his fingers as another loud yelp came from downstairs. Covering him back up and touching his face gently, she left him sleeping.

"There's three minutes left before half time, then I'll make us a cup of hot chocolate," Henry promised, not taking his eyes off the screen for fear of missing a goal.

Tanya kissed his cheek, careful not to block his view of the match, and returned her attention to the notebook.

The column marked *Savings* was woefully blank, the young couple having

Illustration by Ruth Blair.

recently had to spend their Christmas pot on a new boiler.

It meant the cottage was very cosy this winter, but unless Henry got a decently paid commission in the next few weeks, buying nice gifts for family and each other this year just wasn't going to happen.

Putting the little accounts book away, she sighed as she flicked idly through a magazine from the stack given to her by a neighbour. Her thoughts were not really on the features of celebrities she had barely heard of, or recipes with exotic ingredients she was unlikely to find in the Saturday farmers' market, where she bought the misshapen fruit and vegetables that Henry later turned into delicious fruit pies, home-made soups and casseroles.

She was vaguely aware of the sound of the half-time whistle coming from the television.

Henry got up and ruffled his wife's hair.

"I'll make us a hot drink."

She smiled at him and returned to the magazine. Her gaze focused on the article staring at her from the page she had just turned to as a thought began to cross her mind.

They wouldn't have much Christmas money this year, but maybe this would be something she could do for Henry. Tearing the page out before he could reappear and folding it quickly into a neat square, she popped it into her handbag to peruse at leisure on her bus ride to work the next morning.

She wrapped her hands around the hot mug he gave her and breathed in the comforting aroma of the chocolate. Henry had topped it with the whipped cream that came out of a can, and sprinkled mini marshmallows on the top, just the way she liked it.

"Henry?" She spoke tentatively, knowing she had less than ten minutes before the football match restarted. "I've just done the accounts, and we can manage all the bills and everything, but the boiler took our Christmas savings. We can get Ethan a new toy, but we're going to have to cut right back this year."

He turned to her, football forgotten, a look of guilt on his face.

"I'm sorry, darling. I am trying to find work, but no-one wants things done at this time of year. They're all saving for Christmas, too, and unless there is a big storm and fences come down, it seems unlikely I'm going to get going properly again before spring. People only want urgent work done, rather than decorating or building new wardrobes."

Tanya put her hot chocolate down, crossed to the sofa and wrapped her arms around him.

"I didn't mean to make you feel bad about work. It's actually really nice that you get to spend time with Ethan, rather than sending him to nursery full time. It's just we have to be a bit careful about any luxuries this year."

"I had an idea about that. How about we have a limit of ten pounds to spend on each other? A Christmas stocking on a budget. It'll be fun, seeing what we can find out there for as little cash as possible."

A look of concentration crossed Henry's face. The match had restarted but he ignored it.

"I'm already getting ideas. What do you think?"

Tanya's own Christmas idea, drawn just now from the folded magazine page in her bag, might cost more than the £10 limit, but there would probably be a way round it. She grinned at him.

"You're on. It's a great idea."

"And I had a thought about Ethan. Seeing as I don't have much work on, while he's napping each day I could work on making him a wooden toy. I've had an idea for something already, but I wanted to surprise you."

Tanya gazed at the look of boyish excitement on her husband's face. She could picture him as a child, the same wayward lock of hair over his forehead that was already noticeable on their baby when she tried to flatten his blond locks with a soft brush.

People had often noted how much Ethan was already looking like his dad, and they had pored together over family albums, excitedly comparing old faded baby photos of each other with their precious son. No doubt about it, Ethan had taken after his father right from the day he was born.

∗ ∗ ∗ ∗

A warm, weighty and wriggling bundle was deposited on her bed the next morning. She grinned at the tousled head resolutely crawling up the duvet towards her.

Henry placed a cup of tea on the bedside cabinet and inclined his head towards the baby making his way to her.

"I've done his nappy, and his porridge is just simmering. I thought you might like a cuddle before you have to get up."

Tanya sat up and held her arms out to encourage Ethan to increase his efforts to make his way up the folds of the duvet towards her. This was a far nicer way to be woken than the dreaded alarm clock.

Ethan was an early riser, and his cheerful grin and baby chatter seemed to melt away any worries she might have. She really felt she was the luckiest woman alive at that moment.

She snuggled her face into his neck, breathing in that gorgeous baby scent, wishing she could bottle it to savour bit by bit during work that day.

Henry was a great house husband during the spells that he didn't have any work on. The nearby nursery was really flexible, and they only had to pay for Ethan when they needed the childcare.

Any jobs that needed doing round the house were completed without her having to ask, and a cup of tea and warming meal were always waiting for her when she got home. It made sense to run things this way, and although there were people in the office who frowned on the idea of a man staying at home, she knew this arrangement worked for them as a family.

Henry and Ethan were happy, and they genuinely didn't care what anyone else thought.

She kissed both her boys goodbye, Ethan barely glancing up from his breakfast, face smeared with porridge as he attempted to feed himself from the extra spoon Henry had allowed him to hold in his chubby fist.

Meanwhile his dad deftly spooned the majority of it into Ethan's mouth himself. It satisfied the baby; he thought he was feeding himself, as each time the little mouth opened like a beak, Henry would swiftly pop his own spoonful in.

Sitting on the bus a short while later, Tanya extracted the magazine page from her bag.

Smoothing the creases out on her lap, she studied it carefully. She had planned to visit a specialist shop during her lunch break, but keeping under a £10 limit meant a change of plan. However, an idea was already forming.

* * * *

"Do you fancy popping across to the café for lunch?" Her work colleague Denise gestured through the window.

Rain was falling steadily outside and Tanya smiled and pointed at her lunch box next to the computer.

"Thank you, but I've eaten my sandwiches already."

She smiled to herself at the memory of the little note she had found taped to the inside of the lid.

Have a lovely day, Mummy. We miss you already. Ethan and Daddy xxx
She closed down her computer.

"I have a little chore to do, anyway. There's a shop I need to nip into. See you in a while."

Tanya had already decided where she was heading – the other end of town from the shop she had originally intended.

She was grateful for an excuse not to go to the trendy and pricey café that her colleagues often frequented. On the rare occasions she felt that she should be polite and go over with them she only ever had a pot of tea. The food seemed overpriced, and to her, the taste of the lovingly made sandwiches which Henry pressed into her hand every morning by the door far exceeded any delicacy the café had to offer.

The faint musty smell that seemed to pervade most charity shops hit her as she pushed open the door. A little bell clanged as she entered and an elderly lady sitting behind the counter smiled at her.

Tanya glanced into the street behind her, momentarily worried that Denise might have seen where she was heading.

Financed by a husband who worked away in the city, Denise seemed to have a never-ending supply of money, new clothes and jewellery. Tanya was fairly sure Denise would never have allowed herself to be seen in a charity shop.

Tanya straightened her back and vowed never to allow herself to think, no matter her finances, that she was above places like this which did amazing work for various charities. This was one of several similar shops close together in the part of town where rents were cheaper.

The lady behind the counter was no doubt a volunteer, and the shop was busy with several savvy bargain-hunters in it, sifting their way through carefully arranged clothing hanging on circular racks across the main shop floor.

"Can I help you?" The woman behind the counter smiled again at Tanya.

She stood up, leaning on a stick, and with her free hand started tidying a display of Christmas cards on the counter top.

Tanya explained what she was looking for, and was pointed in the direction of a rail towards the back of the shop. After carefully sorting through a number of items, she brought three things to the till.

"I saw it was 'buy two, get one free'." She fished in her purse for money.

"Yes. That'll be seven pounds, please. Do you need a carrier bag?"

Tanya shook her head and picked up a packet of Christmas cards to add to the pile in front of her.

The lady folded the items and placed the cards on top as Tanya dug deep into her handbag to find the little pouch containing the fabric bag she knew was in there somewhere.

She hurried back to the office, head down and collar turned up against the

Christmas Bells

WHAT Christmas joy to hear the bells
When all around are glad Noels!
Church bells ring out across the land,
Each peal rung by a merry band.
On tinsel-covered Christmas trees
Hang tinkling bells, sweet sound to
   please.
In the square stand hand-bell ringers
Playing tunes for carol singers.
Hark jingling sleigh bells in the snow –
It's Santa Claus with lights aglow!
Then after Christmastime has passed
And frosty winter holds us fast,
We'll dream of bells in coming spring –
Dear bluebells warmer days will bring!

– George Hughes.

drizzle, her purchases clutched to her side. Tanya's mind was whirling with the project she had planned.

As she had managed to spend only £7, that meant she had another £3 to find a couple of other bits and pieces. A trip to the pound shop one lunchtime to find something to add to Henry's stocking might be in order soon.

* * * *

Henry was stirring a casserole on the hob as she got home. The savoury smell filled the cottage as Tanya kicked her shoes off by the front door.

She tucked the bag and its contents behind the boots and shoes piled carelessly round the coat rack in the small hallway.

Crossing into the kitchen, she grinned at him.

"I spent seven pounds already on your Christmas today!" she teased.

"Well done." He stopped stirring and left the dinner bubbling gently on the stove as he kissed her. "Ethan and I thought of something for you, too, but we're not telling. I made him promise to keep it a secret.

"Here, let me do that!" he called through as he realised Tanya had changed from her smart office skirt and blouse into comfy tracksuit bottoms and a snuggly jumper. She was loading the washing machine, with Ethan pulling himself up next to her, fascinated as only babies are by the humdrum household chore of putting a load of washing on.

iStock.

171

"It's fine. I'm quite happy to do my share!" she called back, glad that he hadn't seen what she had just put into the machine with the rest of the washing.

She made a mental note to be sure she would be the one to empty it when the cycle finished. Although she could explain away her purchases, it might spoil the surprise she had in mind. She hoped she could manage to do what she planned and hadn't just wasted most of her budget.

Previously her bus journeys to work had been spent reading, listening to music or just watching people come and go at each stop. Now she had a purpose, digging deep into her bag as soon as she was seated, bringing out her project and meticulously following the instructions on the increasingly battered magazine page in front of her.

Lunchtimes now gave her the perfect excuse to avoid the expensive café, as she had something else to occupy herself, barely stopping to take bites of her sandwich each day as her plan started coming to fruition.

*   *   *   *

"I'm wrapping your presents in the kitchen for the next little while," Tanya announced after Ethan was bathed and tucked into his cot.

She put a CD into the player on the worktop and sang along to Christmas carols. Henry had bought a little Christmas tree that day, and they were going to decorate it that evening.

Tomorrow was Saturday; they would go and buy the vegetables for their Christmas lunch – just the three of them for Christmas morning this year – before heading to take Ethan to visit each of the sets of grandparents later in the day.

The holiday allocation meant that Tanya had four days off in a row, not going back to work until Thursday.

She sang a little louder as the strains of "Silent Night" carried through the cottage. She could hear Henry pottering about in the lounge, wrapping whatever he had found for his £10 budget.

She was more excited this year than usual. Somehow, being forced into taking much more care had made it more fun than usual. Scouting the cheap shops for bargains and turning down anything which cost more than one pound had actually been more enjoyable than it had first seemed.

She wrapped the chocolates, football book and preloved DVD she had found in the pound shop, and placed them into a stocking Henry's mother had made him when he was small. She pushed the main present into the top and smiled in anticipation.

Something she had made for Ethan was swiftly wrapped, too. She couldn't show Henry what it was as it might have given him a hint as to what her own surprise for him was going to be.

"Can I come in yet?" she called as she finished.

"Give me a minute!" Henry called back. "And bring the CD player in with you for when we decorate the tree."

Tanya stirred the hot chocolate on the stove, dissolving the grains of cocoa powder and humming along as it came to a simmer.

She grinned as she pictured Henry's face on Christmas morning.

She had two surprises for him this year, and thought she could hardly wait another three days.

∗　∗　∗　∗

"Merry Christmas, darling." Henry smiled at his wife in the soft light as she turned the bedroom dimmer switch on low.

She held a tray of tea in one hand, and his childhood stocking in the other. Placing the tea on the bedside table, she laid the familiar, now bulky item on to his lap.

"Ethan is giving us a lie-in for once. Keeping him up late for the visitors last night worked a treat."

She gazed at him, eyes shining, as he tore open the first package. Two pairs of hand-knitted Fair Isle socks fell out on to the bed. They were made lovingly from the jumpers she had bought at the charity shop, washed, unravelled and then knitted on the bus and during her lunch breaks.

"These must have cost more than ten pounds?" He frowned at her, no doubt thinking she had cheated.

"I made them!" She grinned excitedly. "From wool I got from old jumpers. There was so much left over that Ethan has a matching sweater, too."

Henry reached down by his side of the bed.

"I absolutely love them. I had no idea you could knit! Let me give you mine, then."

Tanya unwrapped a beautifully made, carved wooden box. It opened with tiny brass hinges and was inlaid with a piece of red velvet she recognised from her sewing box.

Eyes shining brightly, she kissed her husband.

"So that is what else you have been doing in the garage all those evenings!"

Tanya had already seen the wooden baby walker with its carefully shaped alphabet bricks that Henry had spent hours making for their son.

"I thought maybe you could use it as a keepsake box. You know, Ethan's hospital wristband, first tooth, that kind of thing."

"It's absolutely gorgeous, Henry, but I might have to commission another one from you."

He turned to her, a puzzled expression on his face.

"I haven't told you what your other Christmas present is." She placed his hand on her stomach. "We're having another baby! Happy Christmas, and don't expect another lie-in this time next year." ■

Haworth, West Yorkshire

WHEN Cambridge student Patrick Brunty changed his name to Brontë in 1802 he would surely have been astonished to learn that it would become one of the most famous names in English literature.

Today the names of Patrick's daughters, Charlotte, Emily and Anne Brontë, and his son, Branwell are known the world over thanks to the novels, now beloved classics, which the young women wrote while resident in the family home of Haworth.

Over the years, many readers made the journey to see the family's former dwelling at the parsonage and to tread the same cobbled streets they trod. The parsonage is now a museum owned and run by the Brontë Society and attracts nearly three-quarters of a million visitors every year.

Haworth has more to offer than its literary connections. The charming town has been a setting in numerous films and TV programmes, including "The Railway Children" (starring Jenny Agutter) and "Yanks" (starring Richard Gere and Vanessa Redgrave). It also hosts a very popular 1940s re-enactment weekend, which takes place in May each year, and sees the streets thronged with visitors in vintage dress. ∎

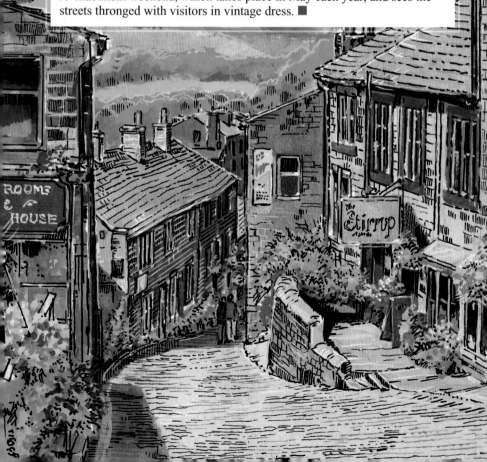